WAYWARD TEMPTATION

WAYWARD TEMPTATION

STARFIRE LAKE
BOOK TWO

VIVI PARISH

Editing by Rebecca Fairfax

Proofreading by Kristina Polacco

Cover Art by Naomi Lane

ISBN | Ebook: 979-8-9859408-2-4

ISBN | Paperback: 979-8-9859408-3-1

✾ Created with Vellum

For readers who love the brother's best friend trope.

Wifey – for all the things.

PROLOGUE

Megan was glad she felt bold enough to wear the light blue summer dress she'd picked out for Caleb's going away party. She'd caught him staring at her a few times, and it sent a delighted thrill through her every time. The lack of embarrassment when he saw her catching his stare, and the desire, heated her blood.

The day had been hot, and though they'd all jumped in the pool for a bit, Megan had changed out of her bikini top and shorts hours ago.

Megan knew Caleb was about to move out of state to pursue a program he'd worked hard to get into. His flight was the next morning, so Megan figured it was her last chance to be brave.

The party lasted hours, with drinks, food, quick dips in the pools, and a lot of laughter. Tucker and the rest of the group had gone to a bar to keep the party going, but Caleb had begged off. They only accepted it once he said he had an early flight. Megan stayed to help clean up, hoping Caleb had the same thought she did.

The cups and plates had been strewn everywhere in the backyard, and it took the two of them a half hour to clean it all up.

Instead of asking Megan to leave once they were done, Caleb climbed on the trampoline and invited her next to him. Her entire body flushed with heat as they ended up colliding a few times before finding a balance.

They watched the stars blink into existence and talked about the future and everything they hoped would come true. Her heart pounded, and her skin was on fire from being so close to him. She could listen to him talk for hours, his voice a low rumble.

Their fingers tangled together as they spoke about their fears and what they hoped to leave behind as they grew, and what dreams they wanted to make reality.

Caleb listened quietly as Megan opened up about how her parents weren't supportive of her dream to become a pastry chef and how it made her doubt herself.

"You can do *anything* you want, Megs." Caleb locked his gaze on her, a soft smile on his lips.

Time slowed. There was only one thing Megan wanted.

Megan closed the space between them and kissed him.

It had been the one thing she wanted to do for as long as Megan could remember. His lips were soft, and he didn't pull away. Instead, Caleb pulled her closer and wrapped his arm around her waist to rest on her lower back.

Caleb swept his tongue across her lips, and a thrill ran through Megan. She opened for him, and a moan escaped as their tongues met. He growled and tightened his grip on her back.

Megan ran her fingers through his hair, the softness lovely against her skin, and dragged her nails along his scalp. Caleb let out a low groan, the sound reverberating against Megan's mouth.

Emboldened by his response and despite the frantic beat of her heart, Megan hooked her leg around his waist and pressed harder against his body.

With a growl, Caleb rolled himself on top of her. Her legs opened automatically for him to settle between.

Megan was grateful she'd worn a short sundress because she could feel his hard cock through his shorts as he pressed against her. She rolled her hips, aching for friction, for him to be inside of her. Any hesitation she might have had about her first time disappeared. Her body needed him, and it was all she could do to stay focused as he found her lips.

"Fuck." The word was a gravelly whisper against her mouth.

Megan looked up at him, her fingers still tangled in his hair. "Yes. That."

"Are you sure?"

It didn't matter that he was a few years older, or that he was her brother's best friend. Megan refused to acknowledge that they would only have tonight, that her heart would break when the sun rose. Only tonight mattered.

She pulled him down for another kiss before she whispered her answer. "Yes. More than anything, yes." To emphasize her enthusiasm, Megan wrapped both of her legs around his waist.

He slid a hand up her thigh but stopped himself before he got to the line of her underthings.

"Oh, no."

"What?" Megan was worried he thought sleeping with her would be a massive mistake and was trying to find a way to tell her.

"The condoms are inside."

"Oh." Grateful, Megan groaned, still desperate to have him. "Then let's go inside."

"I'm glad you said that. I thought maybe you'd change your mind."

Megan laughed and kissed him. She ran one hand down his body until she reached where his cock strained against his shorts. She wrapped her hand around the length of him the best she could through the fabric and squeezed ever so slightly. The whoosh of breath from Caleb made her feel powerful.

"I haven't changed my mind." She gave another squeeze, and his body jolted. "I want you to take me to your bed."

"Who knew my Megs could be so bossy?" He nipped her ear and then licked the spot left sore by his teeth. "I like this side of you."

Her heart skipped a beat at his words, 'my Megs.' But she tried to ignore the flare of hope those words ignited.

Caleb got off the trampoline first and extended a hand to help her. Megan was about to hop off the edge when Caleb stepped in front of her. The look in his eyes was demanding and full of desire.

"Put your legs around me again, Megs."

She obeyed, then hooked her arms around his neck.

"Good to know you can take direction, too." Caleb lifted her, his hands cupping her ass, the fabric of her dress bunching up.

"There are a lot of things you'd be surprised to find out I can do."

A wicked grin spread across his face as he carried her across the yard. "I can't wait."

CHAPTER 1

Packing sexy lingerie in the hopes that the best friend of her older brother would see it was probably not the best way to choose what to bring for a week-long staycation at her family's farmhouse.

Megan was happy for her cousin Rose. Rose's fiancé, Henry, might be a bit bland for Megan, but as long as Rose was happy, that was all that mattered. However, the idea of a week of bonding before the wedding seemed over-the-top to Megan.

She'd even tried to get out of it, saying she couldn't get away from her job at the restaurant. Commis chef, or assistant, to the pastry chef was a time-consuming position, and Megan had worked her ass off to get it.

But Rose had been Rose, and Megan had never been able to tell her favorite cousin no.

Though Megan doubted Rose would approve of Megan's choice of underthings. Or at least of the reason Megan had packed them.

Caleb Jackson.

Her first and longest crush.

The first guy she'd ever slept with.

Her older brother Tucker's best friend.

She might have been in love with Caleb at some point, but Megan had never dwelled on it or looked too hard. If there had ever been a chance for them to have a relationship, it had passed.

That was the reminder she kept on a loop in her mind. She needed it to stave away hope.

There had been a moment last month that still nagged at her, though.

When he said he'd missed the way she tasted.

At Tucker's request, Caleb had crashed at her apartment the night before Henry's bachelor party. Her older brother had no idea about the history between Caleb and Megan, and she wanted to keep it that way. Without a good reason to say no, she'd agreed.

Neither she nor Caleb had gotten much sleep that night. No, they'd spent hours exploring the grown versions of each other's bodies. They hadn't planned it, of course, but any time Caleb had gotten close to her, it felt like her body was on fire.

Megan couldn't stop the memory from jolting through her. *Caleb's head between her thighs. He flicked and laved her clit with his tongue and stroked that perfect spot. Her climax barreled through her as she cried out his name.*

Caleb kissed his way up her body to claim her mouth. He whispered, "I love the way you taste, princess. I missed it."

Her body flushed even now.

Maybe riding Caleb's face while her older brother slept down the hall wasn't the best idea, but it did sound like a lot of fun. Fun had been in short supply in her life recently. She didn't see a problem with a quid-pro-orgasm arrangement with Caleb.

Megan eyed the few pairs of sexy underthings in her dresser for a moment. She grabbed all of them and put them in her suitcase before she could change her mind. She also pulled the shortest two sundresses from her closet and folded them neatly on top of the lingerie and panties.

It can't hurt to be prepared.

Megan swung by the Starfire Lake Books and More shop on her way to the farmhouse, hoping the new fantasy novel she'd been dying to read was still in stock. Her phone vibrated a few times in her pocket as she crossed the threshold, indicating an incoming call.

Abbie's name flashed on the screen. "Hey, Abs."

"Oh! You answered! I thought you were working. I was going to leave a message." Surprise lit Abbie's voice.

Megan waved to Danielle at the register and made a beeline for the table of new releases. "Nope. I'm off this week for Rose's wedding bonding week extravaganza thing."

A quick glance and she found the gold cover of the book she wanted. Fantasy plus romance was always a win in her opinion. If it was as good as everyone said, it would keep her mind off of Caleb in a bedroom right down the hall from hers.

"Oh, that's this week? Tell her I said congratulations, will you?"

"Of course. What were you going to leave a message about?" Megan tucked the book under her arm and headed to the Romance section. It was small and only showcased the authors with the largest followings, but every now and again the owner, who also happened to be Caleb's uncle, liked to stock a newer title. She'd left suggestion after suggestion plus research on how Romance was the largest-selling genre, but things hadn't changed yet.

"It doesn't matter now. I was going to see if you wanted to have drinks tomorrow night but you're busy. I forgot about the extravaganza." Abbie drew out the last word, and Megan could hear the sarcasm.

"I would if it were any other week. Maybe we can do something on Sunday? The wedding will be over, and I'll be back home by Sunday around lunch." Megan chose two romances that looked to be set in a small town, one by a Kait Nolan and the other by a Zoe York. Megan recognized the newest Stacey Agdern book, but already had it on her bookshelf at home.

"I'll bring over cookies and you can give me all the dirty details."

"There won't be any details to give you, Abs." Megan pinched the bridge of her nose, exasperated but trying not to show it.

Abbie was quiet for a moment. "Crap, I gotta run. I'll text you!"

They said goodbye, and Megan browsed for a few more minutes, always making a point to say a quiet hello to the books by her favorite authors.

Abbie's text came through faster than Megan expected.

Is your hottie gonna be there?

I don't have a hottie.

The guy from your couch!

Abbie's response included an emoji rolling its eyes. Megan pictured Abbie making that exact face.

I told you – I don't have a hottie. But yes, Caleb will be there. He's a friend of Tucker's and somehow Tucker finagled him an invite. Tucker is Rose's favorite cousin.

Tucker is everyone's favorite, Megs. But are you gonna hook up with Caleb? Again?

Abbie didn't know the extent of Megan's crush or that she and Caleb had slept together. She'd probably guessed it and wasn't good at hiding her fishing attempt.

There is no again, Abs.

Do you like him?

Megan had no idea how to answer that.

He's Caleb. I've known him forever. He's Tucker's version of you.

Aww, they're platonic soulmates?! No wonder you're afraid to admit you like him. You don't want to get between him and Tucker.

Abbie that's ridiculous.

Megan. I can tell when you're lying even thru text.

No, you can't.

Aha! So you admit you were lying.

Megan put her phone back in her pocket, irritated that Abbie had bested her. Again. Girl was too smart for her own good.

Megan brought her three books up to the register and, after a quick chat as Danielle rang up the books, got back in her car.

Armed with her books, Megan vowed not to let herself get distracted by Caleb Jackson.

Her phone vibrated again. She fished it out of her pocket and saw Abbie's name again. But this time it was a video call.

Megan sighed and answered it. "I thought you had to go?"

"I only have a minute while I walk to get coffee."

"Okay, fine. What's up?" Megan asked.

"I have one quick question to ask you." Abbie's eyes were bright, and her hair was pulled back into a long braid that hung over a shoulder.

"Okay, fine. What's your question?"

"Have you already slept with Caleb?"

Megan knew better than to try to lie to Abbie's face. "Fine. Yes."

"Ha! I *knew it!*" Abbie fist pumped the air.

Megan couldn't stop her smile. "You're ridiculous."

"Maybe, but the fact remains: I was right!"

Megan just rolled her eyes.

"Okay, anyway. Never mind that. Are you going to sleep with him this week? Or try to?"

Megan started her car on and put the air conditioning to high. "No, of course not. Tucker's going to be at the house, not to mention the entire rest of the bridal party. That'd be insane."

Abbie looked confused. "But don't you like him?"

"Why would that matter?" It had never made a difference before. Megan didn't see why it should now. It wasn't as if Caleb lived in Starfire Lake. His life was elsewhere. Her life was here.

"If you like him, you should tell him! And then jump his bones." Abbie laughed after she whispered that last part.

"Wow, Derek being away for so long is really getting to you, isn't it?" Megan liked Abbie's boyfriend. She'd even encouraged Abbie to go on a weekend sex romp with him after Abbie asked for advice.

"You have no idea. But this isn't about me. Why won't you– Wait. Are you afraid that your crush will get deeper?"

Megan blushed. Abbie didn't know the half of it. That night last month had made her realize that she could very easily fall right back in love with him. Caleb was just as thoughtful, bold, funny, attentive, and supportive as he'd been eight years ago.

Except he'd grown into an even more beautiful man, with the body to match – more filled out and toned than he'd been at twenty-three. She'd been nineteen the first time they'd slept together and full of insecurity, but Caleb had been sweet and attentive to such a degree that anyone else she'd slept with since had been a massive disappointment.

If Megan didn't put a stop to the conversation, Abbie was

likely to figure it all out. "That's ridiculous. And I have to drive now so I have to get off the phone."

"Okay, okay. Let me say one thing."

Megan braced herself.

"Follow your heart, Megs."

CHAPTER 2

The farmhouse hadn't changed much since the last time Megan had spent a weekend a year ago. Everyone in the Keating family had access to the house year-round, but Megan had used the house when it was unoccupied to experiment with some new recipes. The kitchen was twice the size of the one in her apartment, which made it that much easier to work and clean.

The oversized living room still had the old leather couches and throw pillows arranged in front of the wood-burning brick fireplace. The built-in bookcases next to it overflowed with books. Aside from the kitchen, that was Megan's favorite thing about the house. Most everyone else loved the fireplace or the view, or even the new hot tub outside on the covered porch. But Megan always found comfort in two places: the kitchen and in books.

However, Caleb Jackson on one of the couches was not a familiar sight. He and Tucker were in the middle of a conversation as she walked in.

Caleb saw her first. "Hey, Megan."

Her heart jumped to her throat at the sound of his voice. "Hi, guys." She gave them a small smile and pulled her luggage over the threshold. Megan heated under Caleb's gaze, and she made a point not to meet his eyes. Tucker stood and said something about going to get a drink. Megan closed the front door and hauled her suitcase and multiple travel bags to the bottom of the stairs and contemplated the best way to get everything up to her room.

The second floor of the house boasted a master bedroom with an en suite, three bedrooms for Keating family members, an official guest bedroom, and a nursery that was converted into a kids' room complete with bunk beds. Except for the master bedroom, the rooms were fairly small. There was also the office on the first floor, which had a daybed for extra guests.

Per the email from Rose, she and Henry would share the largest bedroom until the night before the wedding. Henry would spend that particular night at his parents' house. The Keating family members, Tucker, Rebecca, and Megan, each had their own rooms. Groomsmen Tyler and Caleb would be in the kids' room, and Matthew and Theresa would share the guest bedroom since they were the only couple in the bridal party.

Caleb appeared at her side before Megan could make up her mind about how to take everything up to her room. He grabbed the suitcase and two of the smaller tote bags. "Lead the way."

"Oh! You don't have to do that. I can manage."

Caleb fixed his green eyes on her. "I know you can." He flashed her a smile and the knots in her stomach loosened. "I want to help. Lead the way."

Megan hefted her weekend bag and the small bag from the bookstore and led him up the stairs. Her room was between Matthew and Theresa's and the bathroom. Caleb and Tyler's room was right across the hall, and between Tucker's and Rebecca's rooms.

Excellent. Her brother, cousin Rebecca, and the guy she'd had a crush on for years all in rooms directly across from hers.

Caleb stayed one step behind Megan as she opened her

bedroom door and deposited her bags on the bed. The room was large enough for a queen bed, chest of sheets and blankets at the foot of it, a dresser, small nightstand, and an antique standing mirror.

"Is that a bag from Starfire Lake Books and More?" Caleb put the rest of her things next to the bed and pointed at her shopping bag.

"It is." Megan didn't want him to see her choice of reading material. She shoved the bag behind one of the tote bags. "I stopped in on my way here."

"Go there often?"

"Sometimes." She put her hands on her hips. "Does it matter?"

"Not really. Buy anything interesting?" he asked. Amusement danced in his eyes.

"Nothing you'd like." Megan stepped around him to hold the door open and motion him out, but he'd already dashed around the bed and grabbed the package.

"What do we have here?"

"Hey!" Megan dove for the bag, but he was too quick, and she landed on the bed. She scrambled to her knees and grabbed for the books now in his hands.

He stepped back out of reach. Caleb read the titles she'd picked out. His eyes widened and his expression changed from aloof mischief to something else.

Caleb flicked his gaze from the books up to her and stared for a long moment, the books still in his hands and forgotten. A muscle in his jaw feathered, and he licked his lips in an excruciatingly slow movement.

Megan was frozen in place. Her body tightened as he moved to stand in front of her, and gently placed the books next to her. It was such a simple gesture, even as his gaze never once broke from hers. Her breath was uneven, and her heart beat an unsteady rhythm against her ribs.

It had been too long since any guy had given her a second

look, much less a look that said he wanted to devour her. Megan couldn't take her eyes off his mouth.

A memory from their night together last month flashed through her mind.

His hand pinned both of hers to the mattress above her head. His lips on her neck. He growled in her ear as his free hand found her wet and ready for him.

The mattress groaned as Caleb braced a hand on either side of her and leaned in close. His words a whisper against her skin. "If you want to practice any of those scenes, I'd be more than happy to oblige, princess."

Megan's heart leapt into her throat and her pussy clenched in anticipation. Heat bloomed across her face and chest. His mouth was right there, close enough that if she shifted her weight ever so slightly, she could kiss him.

Worse, she wanted to grab his shirt and pull him in close.

Megan wanted to kiss and lick and suck and grind and ride and fuck him.

She dared to meet his gaze. The look in his eyes went from amused to predatory. A man who could sense the shift in her body.

Another memory hit.

The moment when him spending a night on her couch went from one friend helping another friend to a night of groans and tongues on skin and sweat and orgasms.

She stumbled into the kitchen to get a glass of water. As she grabbed her glass from the counter next to the sink, Caleb appeared in the doorway.

"Did I wake you?" she asked.

"Couldn't sleep," was his only answer. The light that filtered through her mostly closed blinds illuminated the kitchen enough that she could watch as he moved toward her. Megan backed up until she bumped into the counter. He followed.

"Would you like some water?" Megan's voice was breathy as she asked the question.

"No." His voice was rough with sleep. He placed a hand on the counter on either side of her. "That's not what I want."

Megan didn't stop herself as she cupped his cheek with her hand, the scruff on his face rough against her palm.

Then his mouth was on hers and he pulled her against his chest. She explored his back with her hands, no shirt to get in the way of the sensation of his corded muscles bunching and releasing under her touch.

It was wrong to kiss Caleb. Wrong to want him as much as she did. But he felt so good against her, so right, that she couldn't stop.

Caleb rotated them both so his back was to the counter and used his knee to nudge her legs apart. His thigh was between her legs, pressed against her already throbbing center. Megan gasped at the contact, already wet for him, the thin pair of underthings not much of a barrier. Desperate for any kind of friction, she shifted herself against his thigh.

He groaned against her neck. "Fuck. Yes, Megs. Ride me. Use me, and come for me, princess."

Caleb's words unlocked the hold Megan had left on her inhibition and she did exactly as she was told. Megan rolled her hips back and forth, rubbing herself on his bare thigh. Caleb's hands were on her waist, his grip firm but not painful – as if he held himself back while Megan took her pleasure.

She held on to his arms and slid herself along his thigh. He flexed his muscle once, twice, and Megan's legs shook as her orgasm built and built. Her breath came in pants, and soft whimpers escaped her throat.

"That's it, Megs. Almost there."

She altered the angle of her hips, and Caleb flexed his thigh again. The extra pressure on her clit coupled with her slickness and the whispers of filthy encouragement from Caleb sent Megan cresting over the edge.

"That's it. Come for me, princess."

Her body exploded in starbursts of pleasure, her head thrown back as she rode out the waves, and Caleb's thigh.

Caleb pulled her against his bare chest and stroked her hair as she floated back into her body. She looked up to find him staring at her.

"That was fucking beautiful, Megs." Caleb nuzzled her neck. Megan sighed at the soft brush of his lips against her flushed skin. A jolt of pleasure coursed through her when he nibbled her ear and whispered, "Good girl."

Caleb grinned, wide and wicked as if he knew exactly what thoughts tormented her.

Megan swallowed hard and cleared her throat. "I think I'll pass on the offer." She didn't believe her words even as she said them.

"Whatever you say, princess." Caleb stood and used two fingers under her chin to tilt her face up to him. "When you change your mind, I'll be right across the hall."

CHAPTER 3

After dinner was cleaned up, everyone slowly gathered at the large dining table and started up a game of poker.

Megan hadn't played in a long time, but she wasn't worried about the game. They weren't playing for actual money, but for chores during their stay at the farmhouse. Megan didn't care what she won or lost, so the game didn't matter nearly as much as the man sitting across from her at the table.

Caleb.

She needed to focus on something else, anything else. Anything except the way Caleb licked and bit his lip before he made a decision in the game. Or how his forearms were crossed on the table, the muscles toned and strong.

And she really, definitely should not think about the last time his arms had been around her.

Had it really only been a month since Henry's bachelor party? It seemed like it had been longer.

Megan hadn't understood the length of time between the bachelor party and the wedding but there'd been some event Henry wanted to go to – some type of car show.

That one night with Caleb had been intense. It had started

innocently enough – he would sleep on the couch, and she'd spend the night in her bed like usual. She hadn't been able to sleep, and the night had turned into incredible sex and multiple orgasms.

Megan had assumed it was a one-time thing, a repeat of that summer night from years ago. The lack of communication since then had made it pretty clear it wasn't going to happen again.

It shouldn't matter. His job and life were in Vermont. Too far away for Megan to even contemplate a long-distance arrangement.

Then Caleb had to go and offer to replicate a scene from one of her romance novels.

The worst part was that she wanted to take him up on it. She wanted his lips on her bare skin, his hands on her body, and his –

Megan had to pull herself together. If for no other reason than her older brother sat at the same table. If Tucker found out about the history between her and Caleb, or what Caleb had offered only a few hours ago, he'd go berserk. Both of her older brothers had scared off more than one potential boyfriend over the years.

Matthew and Theresa laughed at something, and the sound brought Megan back to the present.

Two seats down from Megan, Ainsley, ever the flirt, propped her elbow on the table and put her chin in her hand. "Caleb, are you ever going to move back to Starfire Lake?"

Megan stared at the cards in her hands. She studied the colors and lines and shapes on the Jack of Hearts and Nine of Clubs.

Caleb cleared his throat. "Uh, I moved back over the weekend."

Megan snapped her eyes up to meet his before he turned his attention back to Ainsley.

"You did? How delightful!" Ainsley leaned forward over the table. "Do you need help finding a job?"

"No, I have one lined up. I start Monday." Caleb glanced at

Megan for a long moment. There was a flash of emotion in his gaze, but Megan couldn't parse it.

"What are you going to do?" Theresa jumped into the conversation before Ainsley could say anything else.

Caleb adjusted so his body angled to face Megan. He looked down at his cards and then up at Megan through his lashes, his lips pulled up into a grin.

"I'm taking over Starfire Lake Books and More."

Megan froze. *Son of a bitch.* "You're *what?*"

He shrugged. Megan wanted to strangle him. "My uncle is retiring and wants me to take over. The timing worked out with some changes at my old job, so I accepted."

"That's great, Caleb. Congratulations," Theresa said from the other end of the table.

"Thanks." He gave Theresa a smile and then looked back at Megan. "I'm looking forward to being home."

Megan's heart raced. How was she going to live in the same town as Caleb after everything? Him living far away had been perfect – it kept her from getting too attached. She'd slept with him last month, taken that emotional hit, because she knew that nothing would ever come of it. There was no real risk to her heart.

One of the reasons she hadn't made a larger fool of herself, like declare her love for him, was because he lived so far away. It could never work.

But if he lived here, in Starfire Lake…there was no telling how quickly she could spiral out of control.

If he was going to be at the bookstore all the time, her favorite place to retreat to besides her kitchen, how would she keep her hands off him? It had been easier when she was younger, ironically, because she hadn't known what it felt like to be kissed by him.

Tucker chimed in. "It'll be good to have you home again, man."

"Are you going to make changes to the store? It's so drab." Ainsley's voice grated on Megan. There was nothing wrong with the store, except their lack of titles in the Romance section.

Caleb's attention moved from Megan to Ainsley. "We'll see. I don't want to make too many changes too fast. I'm hoping to find ways of bringing in new customers. My uncle mentioned that a customer or two keeps asking for us to expand some of our sections. Maybe I'll start with that."

Sly, sly jerk. Megan kept her eyes on her cards. The conversation changed to something Tyler wanted to do during the week, and the poker game picked up again.

Her turn came around in the game. She checked her cards again and didn't have a hand worth playing. "Fold," she said and put her cards face down.

The old wood chair scraped the floor as she stood up to get a drink from the kitchen. Megan tried to ignore the feeling in her back, right between her shoulder blades, that told her Caleb watched her move from one room to the next.

All the mismatched glasses the Keating family had accumulated over the decades lived in the upper cabinet to the left of the sink. Any time a kid's cup or a random mug or glass was left behind at the end of a weekend or vacation at the farmhouse, it automatically became a permanent resident. It was a way to make sure there was always glassware available, and the same policy applied to plates, bowls, and cutlery.

Megan reached for her favorite – a glass shaped like a retro Coca-Cola bottle in a light blue hue – and turned on the faucet.

In the few seconds it took for the water to get cold enough, Megan heard someone come into the room behind her.

"Not a fan of poker?" Caleb's voice came from across the small space, but Megan's body reacted as if he stood right behind her. Fire flooded her veins and desire threaded under her skin.

Megan took a deep breath as she filled her glass. "Not in the mood, I guess." She took a long drink and put the glass down before she turned to see Caleb move closer. His dark green T-shirt highlighted the glimmer of emerald in his eyes, and they were fixed on her.

"Oh? And what exactly *are* you in the mood for, Megs?" His words were a growl, and Megan's body responded to it as if desperate for his precise instruction.

That night at her apartment flashed through her mind again – *his hands on her wrists as he held them against the wall, his tongue on her skin as he worked his way down her body, his cock –*

Megan flicked her gaze down to see the outline of it against his shorts. She hadn't realized that his comment earlier hadn't been a joke. That he did want her again. She looked back up at him. "I –"

Before she could finish her sentence, her older brother walked into the room. "You guys are missing one hell of a game. Tyler's about to have to do all the dishes for the rest of the week."

Caleb turned away from Tucker and hid himself against the counter of the sink. Out of the corner of her eye, Megan watched him adjust himself as Tucker opened the fridge and grabbed two more beers. Caleb's arms were crossed again before the door of the fridge snicked shut.

"Tyler's gonna be pissed." Caleb was the picture of nonchalance as he and her brother talked about the game.

Tucker had a huge grin. "He already is. It's great."

Megan caught the strain in Caleb's voice and made a snap decision. If Caleb wanted her, he'd find a way to follow. She dumped the rest of her water and put the glass in the almost-full dishwasher. "Have fun beating Tyler, Tuck. I'm going to bed – say goodnight to everyone for me?"

"See you in the morning." He nodded at her and disappeared back into the dining room.

Megan added a little sway into her hips as she walked past Caleb to get to the stairs. She paused for half a moment in the doorway and looked back at Caleb, an inviting smile on her lips.

Triumph and excitement trilled through her as Caleb took a breath and nodded in the direction of the dining room as if to say, 'I'll be up soon.'

It wouldn't take long for Caleb to follow, but Megan couldn't decide whether she wanted to yell at him for not telling her the news sooner, or if she wanted to kiss him.

She'd decide in the moment.

CHAPTER 4

Megan opened her bedroom door to find Caleb with his arms braced against either side of the door frame. Caleb may have been on the thin side as a teenager, a healthy but skinny baseball player, but he'd grown into his six-foot frame and filled it out with toned, lean muscle.

She drank in the sight of him, and her gaze snagged on the thin strip of bare skin along his abdomen, visible thanks to his arms lifting his shirt. Megan looked up at him and made her decision.

"Megs."

Megan raised her eyebrow. "Not interested in the poker game anymore?"

He shook his head. "Decided to try my luck elsewhere."

"Would you like to come in?"

"More than anything."

Megan stepped aside as he let go of the frame and came into her room. She made sure the door was locked before she turned to face him. Megan played with the hem of her shirt; it was a pretty blue and listed character names from one of her favorite book series. "I hope you don't mind. I was about to get changed for bed."

"Mm. I would love to help you with that." Caleb moved closer. He wrapped his hands around her waist. His voice was soft as he slid his fingers under her shirt to splay on her bare skin. "I haven't been able to stop thinking about you. The wait was torment."

"Since last month?" She looked up at him as he pulled her closer.

"Mm," was all he murmured. He toyed with a loose strand of her hair. "Since then, too."

Megan wanted to ask what he meant, but Caleb tucked the hair behind her ear and trailed his fingers along her jaw to tilt her face up to his even more.

All thought flew out of her mind as he brushed his lips against hers. The kiss was soft and inviting, a gentle tease. She braced her hands against his chest, the muscles hard beneath the fabric of his shirt.

Caleb moaned and pulled her in close, one arm around her waist and the other between her shoulder blades. The shape of his body was familiar, and a burning need erupted beneath her skin. Megan wrapped her arms around his neck and kissed him back.

Caleb kissed up and down the column of her throat and nipped the sensitive spot below her ear.

Megan tilted her head back to give him better access. She couldn't stop her whimper as he kissed his way along her collarbone. He stopped when he reached her shirt and stepped back, his hands still on her hips and his breathing labored.

"We don't have to –"

Megan pulled her shirt over her head, and Caleb stopped speaking.

Caleb brushed a thumb over the cup of her bra, red with black lace overlay. "You could drive a man to insanity, Megs."

A blush crept along her skin, and she smiled. "That's the goal," she whispered.

He huffed a laugh. Megan reached up to run her fingers through his hair and marveled at the softness. Caleb moaned, and Megan gave a gentle tug.

His gaze met hers, the corners of his mouth curving into a smirk. "Be careful what you ask for."

She grinned in response. "I don't know what you mean."

"I think you know exactly what I mean." Caleb's eyes darkened and he trailed a finger up the side of her body and traced the outline of her bra.

"It's a mystery." Megan let go of his hair and reached for the finger that still played on the exposed skin above the red and black lace. She lifted his finger to her open lips and gave a slow lick, her eyes never leaving his.

Caleb's lips parted and he let out a small *"Fuck."*

Megan burned with need. The gravel in his voice, the desire in his eyes, the feel of his hands on her bare skin – all of it combined to make her want to do wicked things with him.

She licked the tip of his finger and gently pulled it into her mouth and sucked.

"Fuck." Caleb's eyes never moved as he watched her mouth and tongue play with his finger. Megan continued her ministrations for another few seconds, then released his finger with a small pop.

Caleb gripped her chin, firm but not too hard, and he whispered against her mouth, "Get ready, princess."

Megan had hardly a moment to register his hand disappearing before she was in the air. She landed on the mattress, her back against the comforter. Caleb discarded his clothes except his boxer briefs. His hard length peeked over the band at his waist.

There was a new tattoo on his chest, over his heart. It wasn't there a month ago. The black outline of a shamrock with drops of dew, but one drop larger than the others.

"Caleb, please –"

"Please what, Megs?"

"Tell me you have condoms."

Caleb's green eyes sparkled, and his smile widened into a grin. "I learned that lesson a long time ago."

He only ever called her that when they were alone, and she used to hate the nickname. Tonight, it didn't bother her like it used to.

As he leaned down to kiss her, she wrapped her arms around his neck and held him close. He swept his tongue against her lips, and she opened for him. Caleb settled between her legs and took his time kissing her, his tongue meeting hers in unhurried strokes. Megan had never found another man who could kiss like Caleb, who made a kiss seem like the most magical part of physical intimacy.

Her body hummed with need, the need for him to never stop kissing her, and the need for him to stop long enough to put on a condom and finally ease the ache between her legs.

Her hips rolled against him, and Caleb tsked. "Getting impatient, are we?"

"Aren't you?" she shot back.

"I have been thinking about tonight for weeks. I'm going to take my time devouring you. I want to savor every. Single. Moment." Caleb punctuated the last three words with kisses against the column of her throat. He reached the hem of her bra and lifted himself so he could cup her breasts with both hands.

"As beautiful as this bra is, it needs to go." He slid the straps down her arms, and Megan sat up long enough for him to unhook it in the back.

She kissed the hard planes of his chest and dug her nails ever-so-slightly into his back. He pulled the offending contraption off and flung it across the room, where it landed on the cushioned armchair.

Megan nibbled the spot above his collarbone, and Caleb groaned. "Fuck, princess."

"Yes, that *is* the idea."

Caleb undid the tie that held her braid and let the waves fall free. She'd curled it this morning but had braided it before dinner. He ran his fingers through the organized chaos that was her hair. Megan wondered at the expression in his eyes.

"You're stunning, Megs."

She didn't bother to hide the blush that warmed her cheeks. "Kiss me, Caleb."

He leaned in as if to press his lips against hers, but then lowered his head to her breast and pulled her nipple into his mouth.

Megan sucked in a breath and let her head fall back against the comforter as Caleb licked and sucked at her nipple.

It had been too long since she'd had Caleb's hands on her, his mouth on her body. She knew he didn't want a relationship and knew better than to ask for anything more than sex.

Caleb was deft and quick as he undid the button and zipper of her shorts and slipped his fingers under her panties to tease at her already wet core. He groaned and slid a finger inside, and Megan gripped his shoulders. Her hips bowed off the bed each time Caleb stroked that perfect spot and retreated and stroked it again, endlessly teasing and taunting her body closer and closer to release.

His finger disappeared and Megan barely had a moment to wonder where he'd gone before his mouth was on her. Megan had to bite back a cry of pleasure as he swept his tongue up her entrance to flick that swollen bundle of nerves.

"You taste like heaven."

She looked down to find Caleb grinning up at her, his eyes full of wicked delight. She threaded her fingers through his hair. His eyes rolled back for a moment before snapping to meet her gaze. His grin widened into one with feral thrill, and Megan didn't have time to brace herself before he continued to devour her.

Her orgasm built low in her belly, and every stroke of his tongue against her clit sent her closer and closer to the edge of bliss.

"Caleb, please. I'm so close, please. Please don't stop."

In answer, he slid two fingers into her aching core and stroked that perfect spot while he sucked her clit.

Stars exploded and Megan's orgasm rocked through her, wave after wave of pleasure as Caleb used his fingers and mouth to work her through it.

Her body collapsed on the bed, spent and satisfied. Caleb disappeared, and Megan opened her eyes to find him taking off the rest of his clothes. He pulled a condom from the pocket of his shorts. She watched him place the gold foil packet on the bed. Caleb grinned at her then kissed his way up her body until he got to her mouth. She could taste herself on his lips, and it felt like a branding, an entwining.

Megan didn't let the thought linger and slid her hand between their bodies until she gripped his cock, hard and ready, wetness coating the head.

"Do you see what you do to me, Megs?" He gasped when she tightened her grip, and he bent to give her another kiss.

She stroked his length, long and slow, adjusting her grip from softer to harder as she moved up and down.

The muscles in Caleb's arms tensed and shook, and delight lit through her. Megan continued to stroke him, her own body responding. There was only so much she could take before she needed him inside her, but she was determined to give him the same pleasure he gave her.

"I want to wrap my mouth around your cock and lick and suck until you can't take it anymore, Caleb," she whispered in his ear.

"Fuck yes," was his only response. A few seconds later a pillow was under her head and his cock was within reach of her mouth.

She couldn't stop the giggle that escaped. "Someone's impatient."

"You ask, and I deliver, princess. That's how this works." His body was above her head, and he leaned on the headboard. She loved the view of his abdomen, and the new tattoo on his chest. He looked down at her, desire darkening his face.

"Mm, how delightful." She licked his tip, and his cock twitched in response.

A groan escaped him. She did it again and this time swirled her tongue in quick circles around him until she pulled the tip of him into her mouth and sucked once, twice, and let go.

His body shuddered. "If you keep doing that, I'm not going to last very long."

Megan paused long enough to ask, "Do you want me to stop?"

"I don't, but I also plan to fuck you."

She gave a long, slow lick. "We can do both, I think."

Caleb groaned.

"Is that a yes?" She schooled her features into a mask of innocence as she looked up at him.

"Yes."

Megan winked at him before she turned her attention back to his cock. She licked the length of him twice and pulled him into her mouth.

Caleb's hand tangled into her hair. He didn't try to move her head or force movements. He simply held on. The slight pressure from his grip sent throbs of pleasure straight to her pussy. Megan reveled in the power she had over him in the moment. And continued to tease his cock the way he'd teased her with his mouth.

"Fuck, I'm close."

Megan didn't stop. She used one hand to tap on her head, and Caleb's response was a choked, "It won't take long."

She hummed to let him know she heard him, and only a moment or two later, Caleb tapped on her head.

"Oh, fuck!" Caleb cried out. His hips bucked as he came, and Megan kept her mouth on his cock, licking and sucking until he pulled away.

He collapsed onto the bed next to her and pulled her in close to lie with him. He had one arm around her and the other behind his head so he could look at her.

"Damn, princess." Caleb kissed her forehead. "That was incredible. I need a minute to recover and then –"

She put a hand on his chest. "We have all night. There's no rush."

The smile on his face broke her heart. "Mm, that's true."

They lay in her bed for a few minutes, in the quiet. Megan wanted to ask him about the bookstore, about why he didn't say something earlier, but didn't know how to bring it up.

There was laughter from downstairs, a reminder of their need to hide their...whatever this was. Megan tensed as she heard Tucker's voice, but it didn't come closer.

Caleb moved his hand in long, slow circles on her back. She relished the feeling of him next to her, his body warm and familiar, and relaxed into his touch.

Megan had slept with less than a handful of other guys since that first summer night with Caleb between sophomore and junior year of college, almost eight years ago. She'd never found the sense of comfort and security Caleb gave her. Nobody else had ever taken their time with her pleasure, and certainly hadn't savored it the way Caleb did.

She ran her fingers over the shamrock tattoo on his chest and propped herself up so she could see it better. The black outline was thin, and the three leaves were shaded a lovely pale green, with drops of dew scattered throughout.

"This is new."

"I got it last month," he said, fingers playing in her hair. "Not long after we saw each other."

Megan traced the leaves. "It's beautiful."

"Thank you."

She laid her hand on his chest, just below the shamrock. "I've always thought about getting a tattoo."

"Oh yeah?"

"Mm. Maybe a cupcake with icing and sprinkles." As a pastry chef, Megan worked with a variety of materials and desserts, but she had a deep love of cupcakes.

"That would be perfect for you."

"You think?" She tilted her head, hair falling across her shoulder. "I don't know where I'd put it."

Caleb brushed her hair back and wrapped his fingers in it, desire darkening his eyes. "I have a few ideas."

Megan squealed when he grabbed her hips to roll them over until she was on her back again. Caleb situated himself on his knees between her legs. He wrapped his long fingers around her palms and brought her wrists to his mouth one at a time. He placed a kiss on one and said, "Your tattoo could go here." He kissed the other. "Or here."

His touch was gentle, each kiss almost reverent. Megan's heart cracked open.

Caleb leaned forward and pinned her hands on the sheet above her head. He kissed the sensitive skin on her right forearm, just below her elbow. "It might hurt a little here, but it would look lovely."

Tingles cascaded along her arm and through the rest of her body at his touch.

She sighed as Caleb kissed her collarbone near her shoulder. Her blood was already on fire and her body was wet and ready for him again.

"This could be a good place for it." Caleb moved to press his lips to the spot between her breasts. "Or here." He moved down her body to her hips and placed a kiss on one. "Or here."

Megan sucked in a breath as he kissed the other hip and said, "Or here."

"Caleb." She grabbed his chin and made him look up at her. The sight of him worshipping her body drove her mad.

"Yes?"

"You're taking too long."

He chuckled. Actually chuckled. "Tell me what you want, Megs."

"I want you on your back."

"As you wish." He claimed the spot next to her and put his head on the pillow.

Megan settled on his hips, his cock underneath her and already hard. She braced her hands on his chest and slid herself forward and back along the length of him, teasing his head at her entrance.

Caleb wrapped his hands around her forearms and held her steady as she continued to slide and tease.

"Fuck, Megs." He eased his grip, but the muscles in his arms were still tense.

Her grin widened. "If you insist." She sat up, grabbed the foil wrapper, and didn't break his gaze as she stroked him a few times before making sure the condom was on properly. A heady sort of power rumbled its way through her body as she settled herself over Caleb again.

Megan took her time sliding down his cock, inch by delicious inch, giving her body a moment to adjust each time she moved. She straightened up and ever so slowly seated herself fully on him.

Caleb's chest rose and fell rapidly. Megan saw the barely held restraint in his face, the tautness of the muscles on his neck, tattooed chest, and arms. She rocked her hips back and forth and around until his cock hit that perfect spot.

"Oh, yes. Right there." Her words came out as a strangled whisper, and her head fell back, eyes closed.

Caleb lifted his hips and met her thrust for thrust.

"That's it, princess, ride me." There was gravel in Caleb's voice, and his hands were on her hips, keeping her steady while she moved on him.

It didn't take long for another orgasm to build.

"I'm going to –" Megan didn't have a chance to finish her sentence before Caleb's thumb was on her clit, stroking with the perfect pressure.

Moments later, Megan's body shattered apart into bliss and reformed.

"That's it, Megs. God you're beautiful." Caleb's words were strained, and his thrusts became faster and more erratic. He cried out her name and found his own release.

Her muscles weak, Megan swayed on top of Caleb. She didn't protest when he sat up and wrapped his arms around her. His movements were gentle as he rolled her on her back. He slid himself out of her. Megan made a small sound at the loss of him.

Caleb pressed a kiss to her forehead. "I'll be right back." He took care of the condom, dressed quickly, listened at the door for a second and then stepped out into the hall, gold packet hidden in his hand.

As the door clicked shut, Megan stretched. Her muscles protested a bit and then released into the movement. She dressed in her favorite pair of shorts and tank top, climbed back into bed, and snuggled under the down comforter.

Megan was about to nod off when there was a knock at the door.

"Come in," she called, expecting Caleb. She sat up and had to wipe the surprise from her face when Tucker walked in.

CHAPTER 5

Tucker's entrance was more of a stumble than anything. "Heyyy, Meggy." The first word was exaggerated.

It wasn't like Tucker to be stumbling drunk, but that didn't stop her from getting irritated at the nickname she hated.

"Megan. What's up?"

"Nothing, nothing." He bent down and lifted the bed skirt. And then moved over to the closet door and opened and closed it.

"Tucker, what the hell are you doing?" She had a pretty good idea but wanted him to say it out loud.

"Checking for monsters *obviously.*"

Megan was still in bed, the comforter around her waist. "What kind of monsters do you think live under my bed at the farmhouse, exactly?"

"You never know." He winked and left the room.

"Weirdo!" she called after him as he shut her door.

She was in her late twenties and didn't need her older brother checking her room for boys. At the same time, she was grateful he hadn't shown up ten minutes earlier.

A softer knock sounded a few moments later.

Expecting her brother again, Megan groaned, "Go away, Tucker."

"I'm not Tucker, let me in."

Megan hauled out of bed and opened the door to find Caleb with a bowl of pretzels and two bottles of water.

Her face got hot, and she all but yanked him into the room. Megan checked the hallway to make sure nobody else was there or had seen anything. She ensured the door was locked before she turned around to Caleb. "I am so sorry. Tucker was in here looking around."

"What? Why?" He'd situated himself on the bed and put the glass on the nightstand.

She sighed and climbed into bed and settled against the pillows. "I'm assuming he was looking to make sure that none of the single groomsmen were in here to 'ruin my reputation' or something stupid like that."

Caleb glanced at the door and laughed. "Yeah, probably. Good thing he wasn't here fifteen minutes ago."

"That was my thought, too." She took a small handful of pretzels from the bowl. "Thanks for the food."

"Any time." There he was, across from her on the bed, familiar and comfortable.

If she didn't know better, she'd think they could make a great couple. "If you want to go back to your room to go to sleep, you can, you know."

He shifted on the bed. "I can't, actually. My room is uh…occupied."

"What do you mean?"

"Tyler is…busy. He should have put a tie or something on the door." Caleb sat on the edge of her bed. Megan's blood heated, even after everything they'd done earlier.

Then understanding clicked. "Did you walk in on him with someone? Who was it?"

"The lights were off so I couldn't tell. But I will never unhear that."

Megan didn't even try to stop the laugh. "You poor thing."

Caleb took a deep breath and seemed to gather himself. "I didn't mean to wake you up. I'll go and get comfortable on one of the couches in the den."

"You mean the super-small couches in the room next to the office?" Megan looked him up and down. The thought of his huge body trying to squeeze onto those loveseats was almost comical. There was no way he'd get any sleep. "That's ridiculous."

"I've slept in worse spots." He stood and took a step toward the door.

"Wait." Megan paused. She didn't know if they were in a place where they should share a bed for more than sex. "You could sleep here." She patted the open space next to her.

Caleb glanced from her hand on the blanket to her. There was gratitude on his face, but also desire. "Are you sure?"

Megan nodded.

"Use your words, Megs." The command in Caleb's voice was irresistible.

"Yes, I'm sure," she whispered.

Caleb locked the door and padded across the room to the empty side of the bed. Megan tracked every movement. She scooted over to give him more space as he climbed in next to her and got comfortable.

Nerves flooded through her. It had been longer than she cared to admit since a man had slept next to her. Sex was one thing, but to have a man in bed with her while she slept wasn't something Megan did until at least a few months into a relationship.

"Thanks for giving me refuge." The soft smile on Caleb's face wiped away any nerves.

She returned a grin. "No problem. Can't have you sleeping on a couch that's half your size."

"I guess you're right." Caleb laughed. "You know, Tucker told me earlier that you want to open your own restaurant." He gave her a playful shove. "That's badass."

"Not exactly. A bakery." Her brother wanted her to open a restaurant and had tried multiple times to convince her to do it. Megan had zero desire to tackle that particular challenge.

"For weddings and stuff?"

Megan nodded. "That and daily treats, cakes, pies, and coffee. Maybe a few tables so people can eat and drink and talk or read or simply enjoy a few minutes of peace."

"That sounds like a great place. A café with the perks of a bakery."

His compliment warmed her entire body. "Thanks. I have a whole binder of ideas with pictures and recipe thoughts and stuff."

Caleb grinned. "Did you bring it with you?"

"You want to see it?"

"Of course, I do." His enthusiasm made her feel he truly saw her and wanted to support her. It didn't feel as though he was humoring her, like past boyfriends had done.

Megan leaned over the side of the bed and tugged the binder from the backpack she'd dropped on the floor upon arrival.

Caleb pored over it with her and asked question after question and complimented her ideas. He never once made Megan feel as though she was ridiculous or silly for anything. A crack in her heart started to stitch together.

Megan told him everything about her goals, large and small, and the dreams that would turn into goals once the business was up and running.

During their perusal of her business plan and loose sheets of recipes, Caleb ended up next to her with the binder and contents spread out before them on the bedspread.

She leaned her shoulder against his. "You know, I've been trying to convince your uncle that he should open a café in the bookstore. He never went for it."

"Did he say something about if people have somewhere to sit and read, they'll stay all day and leave without buying anything?"

"Something like that, yeah. How did you know?" Megan ate a pretzel and grabbed another small handful.

"He told me the same thing."

Megan laughed. "Thankfully it's under new ownership. Who knows what this new guy will do with the place?"

"Wouldn't it be awful if he wanted to tear it down and build condos, or a parking lot?" He winked. Megan relaxed and went with the joke.

"Ugh, the worst. I'd have to find him and bribe him with cupcakes to change his mind."

"I doubt he'd say no to you, Megs."

She shivered under his gaze but kept her tone light and playful. "Good, because I have ideas."

Caleb's grin turned wicked.

"For the bookstore, I mean," she added quickly.

"Mhm." He licked his lips and Megan tracked the movement.

"Um…" She trailed off, her head empty.

"Maybe we could set up some kind of arrangement. Books and baked goods – who doesn't love that combination?" Caleb snagged another pretzel from the bowl.

"How do you mean? Like run a bakery in the bookstore?" Megan appreciated his offer but that wasn't what she had in mind for her business.

"No. We're not set up for that. Maybe one day. I was thinking more like selling cookies or some kind of small treat from your bakery at the cash register, or even on a small table of their own."

Megan had to fight to keep the shock off her face. "You want to sell my desserts? At the bookstore?"

Caleb smiled, a goofy grin that made the wall around Megan's heart crack. "I've had your desserts. They're incredible. If you ask me, more people should eat them."

It wasn't a bad idea and would be an interesting way to drive customers to her bakery. But she wasn't anywhere near ready for that kind of discussion. There were other ramifications to think about, too, if anything between them went sour.

"It's an interesting idea. But it's thirty steps ahead of where I am, even with planning ahead. I don't even have a storefront yet."

"Consider it an open offer for whenever – if you ever want to discuss it."

Megan gathered her things together and returned the binder to the backpack. She turned back to Caleb. "Your turn. What are you going to do with the store?"

Caleb sighed and looked down at his hands. "I'm not sure. I have to take a closer look at things, but I do know we need to pull in new customers."

"That seems to be a universal struggle."

"I do have a couple of ideas I'd like to bounce off you."

"Me?" Megan asked. "I don't know anything about how to run a bookstore."

He shrugged a shoulder. "Maybe not, but you're a frequent customer." Caleb placed a hand on Megan's thigh, just above her knee. He flicked his eyes to hers as he moved his hand up her bare skin, the movement torturously slow. "Feedback is important."

Megan struggled to get in a breath as she said, "I agree with you on that."

"Is there any comment you have for me right now, Megs?" He trailed his fingers down again, to graze the underside of her knee.

Her desire was reflected in Caleb's eyes, and she opened her legs wider. "Yes, actually. I'd like your fingers higher."

"That can be arranged." Desire darkened his gaze as he complied. Megan's breath caught as he brushed his knuckles against her core.

"Should we turn off the light?" Her voice was barely a whisper.

Caleb growled. "I want to see every part of you, Megs. I want to see exactly what my touch does to you, as I make you come undone."

"Oh." She swallowed hard.

Caleb's grin was wicked as he captured her mouth.

CHAPTER 6

Most everyone was downstairs when Megan finally walked into the kitchen in search of coffee and food. Rose was holding court with the other bridesmaids in the breakfast nook. Theresa and Rebecca had only coffee mugs in front of them, and Ainsley was eating some fruit out of a bowl.

Unfortunately, Ainsley spotted Megan first and called across the room, "Good morning, sleepyhead."

"Morning, everyone." Megan got her coffee and took the empty spot next to Rebecca. "I didn't know there was a confab this morning. Rose, I'm sorry I'm late."

"Oh, no. No confab. We're hanging out."

"Hold that thought, Rose," Rebecca chimed in, her phone up to her ear.

"What now?" Worry creased Rose's forehead. Megan didn't miss the hint of annoyance in her tone, either.

"The florist has a few questions. They left a voicemail a few minutes ago." Rebecca pressed the phone screen a few times and put it in Rose's outstretched hand.

Rose put the phone to her ear and stepped away from the table, Rebecca following.

"So, Meg. We didn't really get a chance to catch up yet. What have you been up to?" Ainsley leaned back in her seat, her bowl empty on the table.

Megan took a sip of coffee before she answered. The caffeine needed to kick in at least a little bit first. "Oh, you know. Work, sleep, repeat. The usual. You?"

"That's not what Tucker said last night, after you went to bed. Is it true you're going to open your own restaurant?"

"No, not a restaurant."

"Something else, then?"

Megan didn't appreciate the prying tone in Ainsley's voice. "Nothing official."

"You're always so secretive. It's just us. You can tell me."

"There isn't anything to tell." Not exactly true. She did have a solid business plan and had even found a great location. The next step of securing funding was intimidating, and she hadn't yet gathered the courage to make an appointment with a business advisor to even ask questions about the process.

"Tucker seemed to think there is. Maybe I'll talk to him about it when he wakes up."

Ainsley smiled and waved to someone behind Megan. "Come sit with us," she called.

Megan's stomach twisted as Caleb sat at the small table, in the seat Rose had vacated.

"Morning," Ainsley practically crooned.

"Morning." Caleb's voice was still scratchy from sleep.

Megan nodded in greeting and took a sip of her coffee.

"Meg here was telling me that she doesn't have plans to open her own business."

Megan rolled her eyes but kept quiet. This week was about Rose. That was where she needed to focus. If Ainsley wanted to do whatever she was doing, that was up to her.

Caleb glanced at Megan, and she shrugged. She couldn't control what Ainsley said.

"That's interesting, because Megan and I were up talking a little bit more last night and came up with some thrilling ideas for both our businesses. But if she's not ready to share anything yet, that's her call."

Ainsley glanced between Megan and Caleb. "Really? When was this?"

"He just said last night." Megan couldn't help the sharpness in her tone.

"I was the last one to go up to bed last night and didn't see you two talking." Ainsley's eyes bore into Megan.

"Didn't realize you were so interested in what everyone else is up to, Ainsley." Caleb's voice was smooth, but the subtle implication was clear enough. Megan was grateful Caleb knew Ainsley well enough to hint at her hatred of being called nosy.

Ainsley scoffed. "I'm less interested than you think, Caleb."

Megan couldn't stop the chuckle as she said into her mug, "Oh, I doubt that." She schooled her features into bland nonchalance.

Ainsley glared at Megan with her eyes narrowed. "You two must have been up *very* late together, and since I didn't see you down here before I went to bed, I can only think of one – well, two – places you could have been having your…thrilling discussion."

Megan's heart pounded against her ribs. But Caleb was smooth with his lie. "We were in my room, Ainsley. So what?"

Ainsley's eyes flared at some secret revealed, and she smiled. "I guess it doesn't really matter." She stood. "I'm going to see if Rose and Henry need help with the scavenger hunt. Try not to both be late for that." She sauntered off.

Caleb sipped his coffee as he watched her walk away for a moment and then looked at Megan. "How did you sleep?"

Megan motioned with her thumb toward Ainsley's retreating figure. "You know that's going to come back and bite us in the ass, right?"

Caleb shrugged. "Ainsley's harmless. She's always been a flirt."

Megan sighed. "If you say so. But this is the first time we've all shared a house with both Ainsley and Tucker here. She may be harmless but she's not stupid."

Thirty minutes later, Megan kept a clamp on her groan as her cousin excitedly paired up the group for the wedding-themed scavenger hunt. Rose was automatically sorting teams into the existing couples, and somehow Megan and Caleb were the only ones who didn't bring a date.

"Meg and Caleb, you guys are Team Four." Rose pointed to both of them and then moved on to explain that Tucker was the referee. He didn't have a date either, but his history of excelling at scavenger hunts usually ended the 'hunt' before most other competitors got halfway through.

Caleb moved to stand a half step behind Megan, his arm brushing against the bare skin of her arm. Heat bloomed where their skin met, and Megan shifted so she stood ever so slightly closer.

Caleb's hand rested on her lower back, and he flexed and relaxed his fingers in a steady rhythm, as if impatient and possessive at the same time. The warmth of his hand seeped through the admittedly thin fabric of her sundress. The memory of the night before flashed through her mind – his hands on her body, his lips on her skin, his tongue between her legs as she climaxed.

Rose continued on, a huge grin on her face, and explained the rules. She held on to a small stack of construction paper, the individual sheets cut into hearts, with the clues written on them.

Megan had difficulty concentrating on whatever rules Rose and Rebecca had come up with. She blushed as Caleb had to reach for the construction paper with their first clue because she didn't notice Rose hand it to her.

"It'll be fun." Caleb said, as he traced a lazy design on her back. Megan's entire focus narrowed down to that movement.

After a few more instructions on where to meet at the end, after all the clues had been solved, Megan let Caleb lead her upstairs. The other groups went off in other directions, heads close and in eager discussion.

Megan's breath whooshed out when he pushed her against the hallway wall and braced an arm on either side.

"That sundress is pure torment, Megs."

Heat pooled low in her belly. She had packed it with him in mind but hadn't expected that level of reaction.

"I'm glad you like it," was all she could manage. Megan trembled as he leaned in to brush his lips against her ear.

"I don't *like* it. I want to pick you up and set you on my cock and have you ride me until you scream my name. *That's* what it does to me."

"Oh." That didn't sound like such a bad idea. The smell of his cologne wrapped around her, leather and oak. She hated to admit it reminded her of home, but it was the truth.

"We shouldn't," Megan whispered, even as she pulled him closer. "We could get caught."

Then his lips were on her neck, and she stopped talking, stopped thinking.

"Let's move to a bed."

They'd gone up the back staircase and their rooms were at the other end of the hall. Caleb grabbed her hand and started to lead the way, but voices sounded from that direction.

Megan saw the open bathroom door and pulled Caleb through it. She closed it, careful not to make any noise, and clicked the lock.

Caleb came up behind her, wrapped his arms around her and pulled her against his chest. Megan leaned into his touch. Caleb slid his hands up and found her breasts as he pressed a kiss to her neck.

Megan rolled her head to the side to give him better access. Caleb trailed a hand down her side and up under the sundress, lifting it out of the way as he slid a finger between the lace panties and her skin and played with her clit, moving in slow, agonizing circles.

Megan reached behind her to run her fingers through his hair and gripped it. Without removing his hand or stopping the teasing to her clit, Caleb positioned them to stand in front of the double vanity.

The large mirror above the counter made it easy to see them tangled around each other. It also reflected the mirror on the opposite wall, which hung above the large garden tub.

"Get your pretty ass on that counter, princess. I need to taste you." Caleb pulled away long enough for her to obey, her legs already shaky.

Megan was careful to move things away on the counter and leaned back on her hands. Caleb lifted the hem of her dress out of the way and slid his finger around her panties again and into her with a groan.

"Fuck, Megs. You're so wet for me."

She didn't have a chance to reply before he licked her.

"I could taste you forever."

The word 'forever' lodged itself in her brain, and she almost stopped him. But then he licked her again, and Megan bit her lip to keep from moaning. She closed her eyes and leaned her head back.

"No, I want you to look at me."

Megan obeyed.

"That's it, Megs. I want you to watch me as I eat you and fuck my hand, imagining it's your perfect pussy."

Megan couldn't do anything except whimper in acknowledgement. Caleb slid two fingers into her and took no time at all to find that magic spot. His other hand gripped his cock and pumped. Caleb kissed the inside of her thighs, one and then the other, and slowly kissed his way to her aching core. He licked her clit, a gentle stroke. Megan shuddered, her body on the precipice of release.

Caleb groaned. The sound pushed Megan closer to the edge.

"Caleb, please. I'm…"

Before she could get the words out, Caleb licked her again. And again.

"Oh my god, Caleb. Yes, yes." Her words were a whisper as pleasure flared out from low in her belly, swirling along her arms and legs, twinging up her stomach and chest and neck.

Caleb groaned a moment later, his hand moving along his cock.

She grabbed his hair and pulled his mouth up to hers to kiss him before she whispered, "I want it in my mouth."

His expression was dazed but he stepped back enough for Megan to slide off the counter. She barely noticed the softness of the rug under her legs. Caleb positioned himself at her mouth.

"Hands on your knees."

Megan obeyed. She relaxed her throat for his cock to slide in and out. His hands tangled in her hair, and Megan let him hold her in place as he took what she offered.

"That's it, princess. God, you take me so well," Caleb whispered.

Pride swelled within her at his praise.

"Fuck." He tapped her head once as warning, and a moment later he found his release. Megan delighted in the quiet moans as he filled her mouth. She swallowed it all.

"Good girl."

Caleb pulled himself away when he was done. Megan stood and leaned against the counter for support.

Caleb pulled her against his chest, kissed her – a deep, slow kiss.

A claiming.

CHAPTER 7

Megan had no problem letting Caleb take the lead with their scavenger hunt clues. Given their detour activity, it was unlikely they would win. But they still needed to play and at least pretend they cared and weren't thinking about continuing their activities in a bed.

"I could taste you forever." Forever. It was that last word that Caleb said in the bathroom that stuck with Megan for the rest of the day – through the end of the scavenger hunt, watching Rose and Henry win, and getting ready for dinner and drinks at the swanky Starfire Lake Country Club, where Henry's family were members.

Megan had spent the longest eight months of her career in the kitchen of the Club before finding her current position. Chef Roger ruled over his kitchen like a kingdom and he was given divine authority. She'd almost quit and considered another career. Instead, the experience had taught her what not to do as a leader.

It didn't help that Henry's family were friends with Roger, which Megan knew meant Roger would make an appearance at the table. Maybe she could slip out to the bathroom when he did. She had zero desire to see him again.

She took one last look in the mirror and stepped into the hall.

Caleb was against the wall next to her door. He smiled as he saw her. "You look lovely."

Warmth spread through her at the compliment. "Thanks. You look pretty good yourself." It was the truth. The dark slacks and light green collared short-sleeve shirt fit him like a dream.

Caleb held out his arm and Megan wrapped her fingers into the crook of his elbow. "Would you like to ride with me?" He asked the question as he led her down the staircase.

"That sounds nice. Thanks." It also meant they'd have an excuse for being alone. Plus, Megan hated driving in the wedges she wore.

Rose, Henry, and Rebecca were all in one car. Ainsley rode with Tucker, Tyler, Theresa, and Matthew. There was space in Rose's car, but Megan was not in the mood to listen to wedding plans and frustrations for the drive.

It was a twenty-minute drive to the country club from the farmhouse, and Megan knew exactly how she wanted to spend the time. She formulated a plan to make sure the other cars left first.

"Oh, hang on, I forgot something inside." She dashed back in and watched from behind the curtains of the front window as Henry and Tucker both exited the driveway.

Caleb had started back up to the house and met her at the front door. "As badly as I want to bury myself in you again, people will get suspicious if we're too late, Megs."

The desire was clear as day in his green eyes. Megan's pussy clenched at his words, and she stumbled over hers. "No, no. We can leave now."

A few moments later, they were in the car and en route to dinner. Caleb reached across the space between their seats to grasp her hand. He brought it to his lips and smiled at her before he pressed a kiss to her knuckles. He twined their fingers together and rested them on the edge of her seat.

It was such an endearing thing to do, and Caleb did it with such a casual grace that it took Megan by surprise. A sense of security washed over her, one that she wasn't ready to examine yet.

She smiled at him. "There's something I've always wanted to try."

"Oh, yeah? And what's that?"

Megan bit her lip, extricated her fingers from his and slid her palm up his thigh to rub his cock through his pants.

Caleb's breath whooshed out, and he readjusted his position in the seat. "Oh, hell yes."

Megan laughed and unzipped his pants. He was already hard, and he helped her maneuver his clothes out of the way. Megan pulled her seatbelt until it had enough give for her to reach him with her mouth.

Megan braced herself as she leaned across the seats and licked the tip of him, and Caleb groaned. Her pussy throbbed, and she wrapped her mouth around his cock. She used her tongue to massage him and moved up and down his shaft, deeper and deeper until she gagged and had to pull back.

"God, I'm not going to last long."

Megan hummed, drunk on the power she had over him. Caleb's hips jerked in response, but he kept the car safely on the road.

"Hang on, Megs. I'm going to pull over. I don't want that pretty mouth of yours to get us into trouble."

She sat up in her seat but kept her hand on him, squeezing every so often. Caleb's breathing was ragged as he pulled into an unlit corner of an empty parking lot.

Megan unbuckled herself. Caleb threw the gearshift into park. Megan all but climbed across the space between their seats and licked his cock.

One of his hands was on the back of her head, the grip gentle, and the other across her back as if looking for an anchor.

"That's it." Caleb moaned. "Take my cock in your pretty little mouth like the good girl you are."

Megan squirmed at the command in his voice. He gripped her ass through her dress, unable to reach her throbbing core.

She didn't stop as his breathing got more ragged and his hips twitched.

Megan slowed for a few seconds, teasing him with her strokes.

"Megs, please."

She hummed and dragged a finger over the sensitive spot beneath where her mouth sucked at his base.

Caleb tapped her collarbone twice, and Megan pulled back far enough to keep the tip of his cock in her mouth and worked him as his hips thrust unevenly.

"Fuck!" Caleb came with a yell.

She didn't stop. Caleb hissed and tapped her again. "Okay, princess," he said, his voice breathy.

Megan immediately released his cock and swallowed. Caleb's hand hooked around her neck and pulled her up to his mouth for a searing kiss, the heat flaring between them like an invisible brand.

"You are incredible, Megs." He kissed her. "I am going to return that favor later tonight." Another kiss, and then he said, "Now get your perfect ass back in your seat."

She licked her lips before she moved. Caleb tracked the movement of her tongue with longing in his gaze. Megan kissed him one more time before settling back into the passenger side and buckled herself in again.

They had a dinner to get to, after all.

· · ·

The dining room looked exactly the same as it had three years ago. Megan had been so happy to walk through it on her last night after all the customers had finished and gone home.

Nothing ever changed at the Starfire Lake Country Club, except the staff in the kitchen. There were servers and hostesses that had been there for years, but the only kitchen staff that had been there longer than two years were Chef Roger and his sous chef, Michael.

But not Megan. No, eight months working under Chef Roger and his 'constructive criticism' that was more akin to an evisceration than anything remotely helpful and she'd almost given up on her career.

She smiled at the hostess, Stephanie, and waved as she turned to go down the hall to the Andromeda Room. Caleb trailed behind. The Andromeda Room was the only private party room in the club and cost a fortune.

But since Rose's parents wanted to have the rehearsal dinner at the farmhouse, Henry had convinced his parents to do something else. They insisted on a sit-down dinner at the Club, of course. Thankfully it was the bridal party and parents of the bride and groom, nobody else. As it was, they were a party of fifteen.

Megan said a prayer of gratitude for the dated carpet as she dashed past the door to the kitchen. She could hear the clang of metal, sizzling, and Roger barking orders. She didn't slow down until she got to the party room. Caleb was only steps behind her.

They weren't the only ones late. Rose's parents hadn't arrived either. Megan and Caleb said hello to everyone, including a hug and peck on the cheek from Henry's parents, Henry Sr., and Patricia.

After a few seconds of small talk, Megan let Caleb lead her to two seats across from each other. Megan sat between Rebecca and Theresa and was grateful for it. Caleb was between Tyler and

Matthew, with Tucker between Tyler and Henry. Ainsley was on Theresa's other side, and Rose on Rebecca's, across from Henry.

Not long after Megan and Caleb sat, Rose's parents – Megan's Aunt Violet and Uncle Thomas – arrived. The servers came around for drink orders and Megan got pulled into another conversation with Theresa.

Still, a large fraction of Megan's attention stayed on Caleb. He talked and laughed with both Tyler and Matthew. She caught a few words – something to do with sports.

Megan tried to ignore the knots in her stomach as she also kept an eye on the door for her old boss. Theresa kept up most of the conversation, and Megan only needed to chime in here and there with a question.

As it turned out, Theresa was a high school history teacher, and worked as the school's junior varsity soccer coach. She raved about Matthew, who taught math at the middle school and coached baseball.

Not long after the entrée was served, Roger made his appearance. Megan's stomach dropped as he swaggered through the door to the Andromeda Room, a smile on his face. Megan waited until he greeted Henry's parents before she excused herself, her legs barely cooperating.

Megan avoided eye contact with everyone as she left the room, hurried down the hall and made the turn that led to the bathroom.

Thankfully all the stalls were empty, but she still chose the one farthest from the door and locked it behind her.

She was able to breathe through the nausea but couldn't stop the tears from falling hot and fast. Megan wiped at them furiously, but they kept coming, and a sob escaped from her throat.

Megan needed to get herself together. Chef Roger had never followed through on any of his threats to her career. She was now in a much better work environment and on the way to achieving her goal. Working for Roger was a painful part of her past, but she refused to let him derail her future. Bastard didn't deserve that kind of power.

Megan took a few more deep breaths, and once her arms stopped shaking, stepped out of the stall to check her makeup.

She found Rose waiting for her, arms crossed and back against the sink. "That man is insufferable."

Megan agreed. "That's one word for it." Ass was another.

"Are you okay? I saw you leave and that's when I remembered you used to work here. I should have asked Henry's parents to pick somewhere else or at least given you a heads-up. I've been so focused on the wedding and didn't *think*. I'm so sorry, Megan."

"You have no reason to apologize. Actually, you coming to check on me was really sweet. Thank you. Hug?" Megan held her arms out, and Rose stepped into the hug. Megan squeezed her cousin, grateful to also call her a friend.

"Okay, I should get back. You're really okay?" Rose stepped back and held Megan at arm's length as she waited.

"Yes. I'll be out in a minute."

Rose nodded and left. Megan checked her makeup and was relieved to find it was mostly intact. Her eyeliner had seen better days, but the new brand of mascara had held up.

She fixed what she could and stepped into the hallway. Megan turned the corner to find Roger leaving the Andromeda Room.

"Shit." Megan tried to backtrack, but Roger spotted her.

"Meg? Is that you?"

She sighed and faced her old boss. "Megan, actually."

"You're looking well. Are you still working in a kitchen, or have you moved on to a more realistic career?"

Rage combined with shame filled her. Rage at his outright dismissal of her skill, craft, and effort. And shame for letting him get to her.

Sure, his food was good, but he'd reached a certain level and decided that was good enough. She wouldn't normally judge someone for finding and staying within their strengths, except

Roger barely did any of the work and berated those that did. He was miserable to work for.

"I'm still in a kitchen and doing pastry work. I'm Commis chef at another local place."

"Hmm," was his response.

Before he could say anything else, Megan started the walk back to the party room. "Bye, Roger."

"Chef," he corrected her.

"Bye, Roger," Megan repeated, with a hand wave over her shoulder. She turned the corner and sagged as she saw Caleb headed her way.

"Hey, Megs. Everything okay?" he asked, a concerned look on his face. "Rose said you were only going to be a second, but I got worried so…"

"You were worried about me?" She looked up at him as he wrapped his arms around her waist.

"Well, yeah. You disappeared without a word. I asked Tucker what was wrong, but he didn't know. Then Rose left and when she came back, I asked her. She told me that the guy that visited the table used to be your boss and he was an ass."

"You came looking for me?" Megan could stare into his green eyes forever. Maybe, just maybe, he felt the same. The only way to find out was to ask him. Later.

"I was worried. You didn't answer my question. Are you okay?"

Megan leaned against his chest, the strength of his arms around her a safe haven. She answered him truthfully. "I am now."

CHAPTER 8

Rose had arranged for each bridesmaid to get a massage and a mani/pedi on Thursday morning, plus a discount on any other treatments offered. Megan was grateful for the gift, but really enjoyed the excuse to get out of the farmhouse and away from Caleb, clear her head.

The Starfire Lake Spa was downtown and had been open for less than a year. The owner, Christine, had also welcomed a new baby only months before the official opening.

The men were off doing their own thing. Megan hadn't asked too many questions.

"Anyone else here think Caleb is sexy as hell?" Ainsley asked the group as they all sat together for their pedicures.

Megan didn't say anything. A pang of worry erupted in her belly. Even though they'd been fucking like crazy the last few days, there was nothing official between them. No relationship to speak of, so she had no right to tell Ainsley that Caleb was taken. Technically, he wasn't.

Megan examined her recently completed nails. The simple french manicure was elegant and would look lovely in photos.

"Is he seeing anyone?" Ainsley asked. "Because if not, I

wouldn't mind a ride on that rollercoaster." Her giggle made Megan see red.

But she reined it in. Ainsley could proposition Caleb all she liked, and Caleb was free to accept if he wanted.

That didn't mean Megan had to like it.

"There's no way he's single, though. Beautiful *and* sweet? He's gotta be taken already," Rebecca chimed in.

Ainsley shrugged. "I guess I'll find out tonight."

Megan snapped her head in Ainsley's direction. "What does *that* mean?"

"Just that I have an outfit he might enjoy. I saw the way he was looking at me yesterday when I was by the pool."

Megan wanted to slap the simpering smile off Ainsley's face. Maybe if Megan shared some details about how Caleb had looked up at her last night, with his mouth between her legs…

Still, Megan kept quiet. It wasn't worth the trouble. For all she knew, after the wedding was over, Caleb might very well go out with Ainsley. She tried to ignore the stab of pain at the thought. He wasn't hers to claim; carrying a torch for him for years didn't make him hers.

There had been no discussion about what would happen when they weren't sleeping in bedrooms across the hall from each other.

Once the wedding was over and Rose and Henry happily married, Megan and Caleb would go back to their separate lives.

It was the best thing for both of them. He would put all of his attention on the bookstore, and she could get back to focusing on her career and finding a way to open her own bakery.

Running her own business had always been Megan's goal. The building two doors down from the spa was still vacant and used to be a restaurant; she'd seen the sign as they'd parked on the street in front of it. She'd have to make some inquiries about the building before she could do anything, of course, but it was in a good location. The previous restaurant had closed when the owners retired and none of the kids wanted it, and the economy had been in a downswing, so nobody wanted to take on such a risk.

Her parents tried for years to get Megan to follow a different career path, but the kitchen and baking had been her dream since she was a kid standing in front of a bakery display, realizing people *made* them.

If she was going to finally make it happen, she couldn't afford any distractions. She owed it to the younger version of herself and owed it to who she was now to keep her head down and focused.

No distractions meant no Caleb. After this week. She could give herself these last two days. Rose was getting married on Saturday. Which meant Megan had two days and nights left to be distracted.

As long as Ainsley didn't get her hooks into Caleb.

"You brought lingerie to the bonding week before my wedding?" Rose's shock was clear enough, and loud enough that it brought Megan back to the conversation.

Ainsley scoffed at Rose's surprise. "Why not? There are single groomsmen with us, aren't there?"

"It's bold, that's for sure," Rebecca said.

"Not to mention cliché," Megan said before realizing she said it out loud. She tried to find anything else to say but Ainsley cut her off.

"Maybe, but when was the last time *you* bought lingerie, Megan?"

She had to grind her teeth to stop herself from telling Ainsley that she too had brought lingerie to the farmhouse, and with the intention of having Caleb take it off her. Exactly like he did last night. Ainsley didn't need to know any of that.

So, Megan kept her mouth shut. She didn't know Rose's college roommate all that well and was happy to leave it that way.

"That's what I thought."

"No fighting, guys. Come on," Rose piped up. Ainsley made a show of sitting back into her seat and continued to stare daggers at Megan.

Great.

Megan did her best to ignore Ainsley for the rest of their appointment at the spa all the way through to dinner. Instead, she focused on getting to know Theresa better. She hadn't spent much time with Rose's newer friend.

If only Ainsley would stop following Caleb around like a puppy. She'd insisted on helping him with the barbecue and found every possible reason to touch his arm.

Megan had to remind herself for the thirtieth time that day that Ainsley could flirt with whoever she wanted, and Caleb could turn her down or accept as he pleased. Of course, if he did say yes to Ainsley's propositions, it would make him a jerk and she would never sleep with him again.

Theresa was sharing a story about how she and her boyfriend, Matthew – also a groomsman – had met. Megan smiled and tried to listen to Theresa's words, but her gaze kept drifting to where Ainsley sat practically on top of Caleb on the other outdoor couch. She tried to catch Caleb's eye, but he was in conversation with Tucker, and Megan really didn't want Tucker's attention.

"But he helped me figure out statistics, so the least I could do was take him out for coffee, you know? The rest was history." Theresa laughed and Matthew beamed at her like she was the sun. The love on Matthew's face hit Megan like a truck, and suddenly the deck seemed too crowded.

"That's so sweet. You guys are lucky to have each other." She took a sip of her water and excused herself to get more.

Megan had to pass Caleb and Tucker – and Ainsley – on her way inside. Caleb looked up at her as she went by, but her chest felt as though it would cave in at any moment.

She couldn't get her heart to calm down or her lungs to cooperate. It didn't make sense. She left her glass in the sink and went up to her room, taking the steps very deliberately because her legs felt like jelly.

After she finally made it to her room, Megan sank down against the bed, closed her eyes, and concentrated on the in and out of her breath. In for one, two, three seconds. Out for one, two, three seconds.

The counting helped, and her heart no longer felt as though it would implode, but the invisible pain still ached. Tears fell, and she choked back a sob. Spending even a few days with Caleb knowing there wasn't a chance for them hurt more than she'd anticipated. The sex was fun, but she'd always wanted more.

There was a small knock at the door, followed by Caleb asking if he could come in.

Megan wiped away tears and took a steadying breath. "Sure," she called.

Caleb stepped in and made sure to lock the door behind him. "Hey, what's going on?"

"I wanted a little bit of quiet." She couldn't meet his eyes. "It was getting a little bit…much, out there. That's all. I'm okay, really."

Caleb crouched next to her, a skeptical look on his face. "Mind if I sit?"

He'd always been able to see through her. She shook her head. He took a seat on the floor close enough that their shoulders touched. Megan leaned against him, her head on his shoulder.

"Thanks for coming to check on me."

"It's what I do, princess." Caleb kissed the top of her head and pulled her closer. He'd always paid attention to her mood and changes in her emotions when they were younger.

The realization struck hard.

Anytime one of her brothers or one of their friends said something to upset her in front of Caleb, he was the first to defend her. He'd also always been the one of Tucker's friends to greet her first whenever he came over.

Megan couldn't believe she'd never noticed it before.

His attention.

Maybe she'd been too preoccupied with trying to hide her feelings that she never saw his. It was plain as day when she stopped to look at it.

Still, she wasn't ready to ask him about it. What if she was seeing something that wasn't there only because she wanted to? So, she fell back on their unspoken agreement for the week. The one piece of him she could have while they were here together.

She stood. Megan met his gaze, and the desire in it matched her own and made her feel powerful and sexy. Caleb didn't take his eyes off her as she pulled her shirt over her head and stepped out of her sandals.

He stood in a fluid motion and drew her in for a kiss, one hand on her bare lower back. He trailed the other in a smooth line up her side, curving around her bra, and up her neck to cup the back of her head.

The kiss was passionate, but Caleb's movements were slow and deliberate. As if he knew she needed reassurance that his attention the entire evening had been on her and no one else.

Megan sighed and all the tension in her body eddied out. She slid her fingers under his shirt and traced her nails along his back. He stepped back long enough to yank it off and toss it aside. Then he was on her again, his hands on either side of her neck tilting her face up to him. He swept his tongue across her lips, and he groaned as she opened for him.

The sound unlocked whatever hold she had on herself. The need to have him inside her again was almost too much. She broke away from the kiss to take off her skirt and climb on the bed. But Caleb grabbed her hands.

"You don't do that. *I* do that." His eyes darkened before he kissed her again. "Hands behind your back. No touching."

Megan shivered in anticipation, need building, but she obeyed, her hands clasped together behind her as instructed.

Caleb leaned in to kiss her neck, and Megan's head rolled back, her eyes closed.

"You are stunning." He placed another kiss on her shoulder and then one on each breast, and another on her belly.

"Eyes on me, princess." His voice was rough and commanding. She opened her eyes to see Caleb on his knees in front of her. Her breath caught at the sight of him, and desire pulsed through her. His strong hands gripped each of her hips and held firm.

The need to run her fingers through his hair was almost enough to make her break his first command, but she squeezed her arms instead.

His eyes never wavered from hers. Electricity danced along her skin as he traced a line from her hips to cup her ass under the skirt. The tremble of his fingers when he reached the lace edge of her panties betrayed his tenuous grip on his control.

Caleb groaned her name into her belly and then nipped at her hip. Megan kept her grip on her arms, her own restraint hanging by the loosest of threads.

Her legs shook when Caleb hooked his fingers under the lace edge of her underwear and slid two fingers along her entrance.

"Caleb," she whispered.

His gaze flicked up to meet hers. "I love how wet you are for me." He continued to play with her, tracing the little bundle of nerves and then down her entrance. Megan's legs shook, and heat and need built and built as he teased. She reached for him, and his fingers disappeared. He stepped away from her so quickly she teetered in place.

"No touching." He waited for her to put her arms behind her back again. She obeyed, desperate for his hands on her again.

Instead of resuming his position, he stepped so close their bodies pressed together. He braced one hand on her lower back and lifted the hem of her skirt.

Caleb leaned down as if to kiss her, and Megan tilted up to meet his lips, but he stayed far enough away that she couldn't reach. She gasped as he slid one finger inside her and then another. Megan rocked her hips against his hand, the need for friction, for release, almost too much to bear.

"Caleb." His name was a plea on her lips.

He let out a soft laugh and dipped his head so that his nose brushed her neck. "Is there something you want, princess?" Caleb played gentle circles on her clit. It was enough pressure to drive her mad, drive her to the edge of release, but not cross that dam-breaking threshold.

"Please," was all Megan could manage. His hard cock pressed against her hip, and it twitched as she continued to roll her hips in her body's search for release.

"I like it when you beg." Caleb licked her neck in one long, slow motion, and nipped her ear. Each touch and bite sent shocks of pleasure through her body, but it wasn't enough.

A small whine escaped from her throat. Megan couldn't stop it.

Caleb nibbled the sensitive spot between her neck and jaw, ignoring her protest completely. He still worked magic with his fingers, stroking and working her along the edge between her building need and orgasm.

"Look at me, Megs." He gripped her chin and turned her head to face him. Megan's legs shook as her orgasm danced away out of reach once again.

"Caleb," she pleaded.

He brushed a kiss against her lips and whispered, "Look at me. I want to watch as you come for me."

A small sound escaped Megan. Caleb didn't pull back as her orgasm built and built and shattered through her.

Caleb kissed her as wave after wave of her orgasm rocked through her.

He slipped his fingers out of her and guided her to the bed.

She didn't trust her legs to hold her up and was grateful for his help.

Megan closed her eyes and focused on her breath. In. Out. In. Out. "That was– Wow," she said, once she was able to form a coherent sentence.

Caleb had lain next to her, on his side with his arm propped to keep his head up. "I could watch you orgasm every day."

Megan's heart stuttered. "I don't think I could say no to that."

Caleb chuckled and kissed her forehead.

The problem was her feelings. She couldn't see a way to be fuck buddies for a long period of time while keeping her heart protected.

She needed answers. *Fuck it.* Megan rolled to face him, her hand keeping her head up, and adjusted her clothes so they weren't lumped under her side. "I need to ask you something."

"Anything."

Megan started with the easiest questions. "Why didn't you tell me you were going to move back to town? Or that you were taking over the bookstore?"

"It all happened after that night at your apartment. I didn't want to say anything because I wasn't sure if you wanted more than that one night or to never see me again. And then it happened so fast. Between giving notice, packing, moving, it was a lot." He took a breath. "I'm sorry I didn't tell you."

Megan didn't know what to make of that. A lot of it sounded like an excuse – something to say to a hook up to blow them off. That had never been Caleb's style. "Thank you. For the apology, I mean."

Caleb smiled at her, and it was like the entire room warmed. "Anything else?"

Yes. "I don't know how to say it."

"Okay. Can I tell you something instead?"

Megan nodded.

"I meant it when I said I haven't been able to stop thinking about you. I don't want this week to be the only time we spend with each other."

"Me neither." Megan grinned. Hope bloomed but she kept a tight leash on it. "What are you hoping for after the wedding?"

"I'm hoping you'll go to dinner with me."

"I'd like that." Megan leaned across the small space to kiss him again but froze when she heard Tucker's voice from the hall.

Caleb put a finger to his lips in silent direction, and Megan nodded.

She couldn't make out what he said, but she heard Ainsley's response, clear as day. "You don't really expect to find them together, do you? I mean, really, Megan and Caleb? Talk about a mistake. Come on, Tucker, we should go make our own fun – take a page out of their book…if that's even what they're doing."

Megan rolled her eyes and could picture Ainsley hanging all over Tucker in the hallway. She'd been trying to get Tucker into bed for years and had failed each time and still didn't get that he had no interest.

Megan sat up and moved to the edge of the bed but didn't stand.

Tucker's voice was clearer, and closer, and Megan could tell he was pissed. "You're the one who insinuated something's going on between them, Ainsley. Don't try to back out of it now."

Ainsley huffed. "Even if they are sleeping together, who cares?"

"They'd better not be." Venom laced Tucker's voice. "I warned him years ago to stay the hell away from Megan. He swore he had no interest. Bastard better not be going back on that now."

Megan's heart dropped as she twirled to meet Caleb's gaze. His green eyes were filled with shame.

She couldn't speak, couldn't…couldn't think. She opened her mouth to say something, anything, but no sound came out. Caleb shook his head and pointed to the door.

Tucker was still out in the hall.

Red-hot anger swelled up from her belly and into her chest, filling the new cracks in her heart.

"Get out," she seethed.

"Please," he started. "Let me explain."

Megan stood up when he reached for her. She didn't give a damn if Tucker found out. Not anymore. "No." Megan unlocked the door and opened it. "Get out."

Tucker and Ainsley stood across the hall, in Caleb and Tyler's room. Tucker stormed across the hall and made as if he would cross into her room.

Megan's lungs couldn't get enough air. Her older brother, the one she trusted to have her back even with his overprotective bullshit, had gone behind her back and threatened... She could hardly wrap her mind around it.

She glared at her brother. "Don't even think about it."

"If he touched you, I swear I'll kill him." Rage contorted Tucker's features. Megan didn't cower or shrink from her older brother. Growing up with two older brothers meant Megan had learned to go toe-to-toe with anyone. She knew Tucker loved her, but he had gone so far beyond the line of brotherly protection that Megan was tempted to drop-kick him across the room.

"Shut up. You had no right to threaten him, now or back then."

"Megan, it's my job to protect you."

"The hell it is! Don't speak to me as if I'm some simpering little thing that can't handle her own business."

Tucker motioned to Caleb behind her. "Obviously you can't if you've been fucking my best friend."

Fury erupted in Megan's chest. "It's none of your damn business who I do or don't sleep with, Tucker. It has never been and will never be any of your business. Stay out of it."

Ainsley stepped into the hall. "Let's go, Tucker. We don't want to wake up Rose and Henry."

Their room was right down the hall.

Megan glared at both her brother and Ainsley as the latter led the former back to the first floor.

Megan turned to face Caleb, her heart breaking. "Is *that* why you never called me after that first night? All these years I spent wondering, and this *week* we spent hiding, and it was all because *Tucker* told you to stay away from me?"

Tears filled her eyes as she waited for Caleb to answer.

"Megs –"

Pain sliced through her heart at the name only he ever used. "Don't call me that. Not anymore."

Shame filled his eyes as he corrected himself. "Megan. I'm sorry. I was stupid. Please, don't let something stupid come between what we have."

"There's nothing to come between. We don't have anything anymore, except memories. Get out."

Caleb opened his mouth as if to say something else but closed it again and left.

Megan locked the door behind him.

CHAPTER 9

"I can't believe Tucker did that. What an asshole." Abbie's voice was anything but calm, and even over the phone Megan knew her best friend would be gesturing angrily as she spoke. She'd sent Abbie a text with some of the details and her friend had called immediately.

"I mean, yeah okay, he's your older brother and he wanted to protect you – fine. But to go as far as threaten Caleb to stay away from you? That's so…movie-level cliché and *stupid*. There were so many other ways he could have handled it."

Megan knew Abbie meant well, but fury still boiled in Megan's gut. "He should have stayed out of it."

"That would have been a good idea, too." Abbie was quiet for a few extra moments. "Meg?"

"Yeah?"

"What do you think would have happened if you hadn't overheard Tucker when you did?"

The memory of Caleb asking her to dinner flashed through her mind. She'd been more than ready to sleep with him again in that moment, like they'd been doing all week.

"What do you mean?"

"Well, what was the plan for after the wedding is over?" The gentleness in Abbie's voice suggested the hesitation she had in asking.

But Megan didn't have an answer. Not a real one.

She'd barely said yes to dinner with Caleb before everything came to light. Megan wanted to bring up the possibility of more but was afraid he'd say that he didn't want anything serious, and he'd certainly never mentioned the topic.

"I don't know." It was the truth. "We didn't really talk about it." No, instead they'd spent their precious stolen moments grasping frantically for pleasure.

Megan sighed. "We probably should have talked about it."

"Yeah, probably. But also, maybe it's okay that you didn't."

"What do you mean?"

"Well, if you had and decided to keep seeing each other or were getting serious or whatever, what do you think would have happened when Tucker found out?"

"Probably the same thing that happened." Megan thought it through. "But also, probably worse at that point."

"So, better to know now, right? Before it got serious?"

"Right."

Except it had always been serious for Megan. She'd been half in love with Caleb for the last decade, no matter how hard she tried not to feel that way. No other guy she dated had ever measured up, and she'd tried to settle for less, to convince herself that it wasn't actually settling. But it never lasted longer than a few months, maybe a year.

Megan had no idea how her heart was going to recover from the double betrayal. It didn't seem likely to happen any time soon.

But Abbie didn't know any of that.

"What are you going to do now?"

Megan wiped the last of the silent tears away and took a shaky breath. "I'm going to cry a little more, shower, get ready for bed and then tomorrow go to the rehearsal and dinner and be a great bridesmaid for Rose."

There was no denying that more tears were on the way, and Megan didn't bother hiding it. She would let herself fall apart tonight. Then tomorrow she'd shove aside her heartbreak and focus on Rose.

She would wait until her cousin had her happily-ever-after; then Megan would figure out how to pick up the pieces of her own heart.

CHAPTER 10

Megan's room was too small. The entire night she kept opening her eyes and imagined the walls getting closer and closer. Finally, she left the bedside light on, hoping for actual sleep.

Even with the claustrophobic illusion handled, Megan barely slept.

There was too much information and emotion roiling through her to be able to rest. She'd eventually forgive Tucker for his stupid older-brother-protection bullshit. Keyword there was 'eventually.' For now, he would remain firmly on her shit list. Irritating, overbearing, boundary-crossing, protective moron.

But the real pain that kept her awake was Caleb. Megan had spent literal years wondering what would have happened if she'd told him how she felt. There was no way to know what could have happened if she hadn't been so afraid of rejection.

She'd always thought herself too much of a coward. Even after she'd seen him at random times after that first summer night together, she'd mentally kicked herself for doing and saying nothing.

Instead, she'd come to find out Caleb was just as cowardly. Oh sure, he'd sleep with her in secret, but wouldn't fight for her – wouldn't take that risk against Tucker.

If he wouldn't do it, why should she? If Caleb had never thought she was worth the risk of Tucker finding out and making good on whatever threat, then why should Megan bother with him at all anymore?

She would have to wash her hands of Caleb and any notion of a romantic relationship she might have developed over the last few days. She'd been such a fool this whole week.

Megan waited until the clock showed seven in the morning before she dressed and went to the kitchen for coffee. It was going to be a long day, and she'd need as much caffeine as possible to get through the rehearsal this afternoon.

One small blessing was being partnered with Tyler for the procession. No reason to even have to look at Caleb today.

She found Rebecca in the kitchen, a frown on her brow as she scribbled furiously on a sheet of paper. "Morning," Megan said.

"Hi," was all Rebecca said.

Megan made her coffee and stood at the island across from Rebecca. "Do you need help with anything?"

"I think I have it under control," Rebecca started. "But I wouldn't mind having some company." Rebecca smiled at Megan, and Megan realized how in her own head she'd gotten over the last few days. She'd love to spend her morning with her cousin.

Grateful for the excuse to get out of the house and spend the time with Rebecca, Megan decided to spoil them both. "I'm in. And I'm buying us some more coffee. Because this" – she motioned to her mug and at the half-full one by Rebecca's arm – "is nowhere near what we'll need to get everything done on that list."

· · ·

Two hours later, Rebecca pulled her SUV into the driveway of the farmhouse. They were able to get everything on Rebecca's list except for safety pins, but Megan had brought some with her.

As Megan and Rebecca unloaded the bags from the car to the spacious living room, Theresa and Ainsley came in to help. Megan was going to stay and help organize but Rebecca ordered her to take a nap.

"The girls and I have it under control. Go get some sleep."

Ainsley's head perked up from the bag she was sorting at that, eyes narrowed for a second before saying, "Don't forget to set an alarm!" Her tone and smile had never been more fake cheery.

Megan ignored the not-so-subtle dig and climbed the stairs. She did set an alarm but not because of Ainsley.

The moment her head hit the pillow, exhaustion won and pulled Megan into a fitful sleep.

Too quickly, the alarm blared, and Megan smacked it off. The last thing she wanted to do was stand in a beautiful church and watch two people madly in love with each other practice their promise to fight for each other and their marriage, to put each other above all else. And to do it while standing a few feet from Caleb so soon after everything had come to light was a special kind of torment.

But the next almost forty-eight hours were not about Megan or her broken heart. She refused to be so selfish. She took a deep breath and pulled herself out of bed. Her broken heart could wait until Sunday when she was home.

Until then, blinders on.

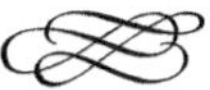

CHAPTER 11

The church was lovely, with a few stained-glass windows and a red brick exterior. Megan had driven by herself, after a feigned excuse about a quick errand. She'd left ten minutes before they were all supposed to leave.

It was a beautiful summer day, if hot. The blue sky dotted with white clouds over the top of the pretty church was so picturesque it felt like a mockery of her pain. As if the universe simply did not care about her broken heart. Rude.

The inside of her car was cool, and she spent the extra few minutes of alone time doing some deep breathing.

One by one, the others arrived, and Megan stepped out to meet everyone and go inside. Caleb tried to catch her arm, but Megan dodged him and climbed the few steps into the building.

Rose gathered everyone inside and introduced Pastor Melissa, who wore a long black skirt and tank top that showed off the multiple tattoos on her arms. Megan didn't recognize her, though that didn't say much because her attendance at services had lapsed a long time ago.

"Melissa is the new lead pastor," Rose explained.

Melissa smiled, and Megan liked her immediately. An aura of

calm authority emanated from the woman, and everyone in the bridal party quieted down.

"Welcome to the Starfire Lake Church. As Rose said, I'm Pastor Melissa, but I usually go by Mellie. We're going to keep this quick and simple. Can everyone head to the back of the Sanctuary and line up in your procession order, please? We're going to practice walking in a straight line, and we're all going to pretend like we've done this sober many times."

Rose spoke up. "Oh, right. We changed the partners around. Tyler, you're now with Ainsley, and Caleb, you're with Megan. Theresa you're still with Matthew, and Tucker and Rebecca – you're still paired up."

Pastor Mellie looked at everyone, and when nobody moved, said, "Okay, kids, time to line up."

Caleb to her right, Megan stood behind Rebecca and watched as Pastor Mellie helped Rose decide the final order of the bridesmaids and groomsmen. She instructed them to stay put and went to speak to both sets of parents about their roles.

Caleb shifted his weight and dropped his head to whisper, "Can we please talk, Megs?"

"There is nothing to talk about, so, no," she whispered back.

"I disagree."

She rolled her eyes. "You would."

"What does that mean?"

Megan almost, almost launched into a tirade that spelled out exactly how entitled and selfish he was being by requesting more of her time and emotional labor but stopped herself.

It was the wrong time and definitely the wrong place for any kind of conversation between them.

"Focus on the rehearsal, okay?"

"And then you'll talk to me?"

Megan thought she heard desperation in his voice.

"No," Tucker cut in. He turned to face Caleb. "Are you seriously bothering her right now?"

Megan stepped between them, her back to Caleb. "*You* don't get to say anything right now either, Tucker. Do not, for the love of – well, God, make a scene in this church during Rose's rehearsal or I'll tell Dad what *actually* happened to his Mustang."

Tucker's face blanched. He gave Caleb another glare and resumed his post next to Rebecca. Megan stepped back to her place in line and continued to ignore Caleb's existence except when absolutely necessary.

Maybe she should tell her dad that his beloved 1987 Mustang ended up in the lake not because of joyriding thieves but Tucker. She passed the time contemplating the different ways her dad would skin Tucker. It was enough distraction to get her through the rehearsal, but every time she held Caleb's arm as they all practiced the processional, her skin burned.

Dinner at the farmhouse would be its own challenge, but one step at a time. Literally, it seemed.

Rose's parents had dinner catered to the farmhouse by the restaurant Megan worked for, Stardust Restaurant.

The caterers arrived not long after everyone got back from the rehearsal, and dinner was a delicious spread of carved meats, pasta, chicken dishes, and sides. Megan's plan was to make her escape right after dessert, which was a tier of cupcakes of varying flavors, but all decorated with lavender buttercream and edible glitter.

Megan had gone over the design with Rose last week to confirm everything but hadn't actually made any of the desserts. She checked on them before dinner was over, and they were beautiful.

The conversation during dinner jumped around from the wedding to honeymoon plans to the housing market to possible job changes and was distracting enough that Megan was able to ignore both Caleb and Tucker.

She'd chosen a seat between Theresa and Rose and focused on her food while listening to everyone. It was when Theresa leaned on the table and asked Rose a question that Megan paid attention.

"Rose," Theresa started. "How did you know Henry was The One?"

"What?" Rose looked like a deer in headlights.

"Well, you know, when did you know you wanted to marry Henry?"

"Oh." Rose took a moment before she answered, clearly perplexed. "Uh, I don't think I had a moment of knowing. We've been together for a while and we love each other and I'm happy, so when he asked, I said yes."

Megan caught the flash of disappointment on Theresa's face before she covered it with a smile. "That's so lovely." She turned back to chat with Ainsley on her other side.

"You okay, Rose?" Megan leaned in and whispered low enough so only her cousin could hear.

"Nervous, I think."

"That's normal. Weddings are long days with a lot going on. It's overwhelming."

Rose smiled but her eyes were downcast at her plate. "It's not the wedding." She frowned.

There was so much laughter and chatter going on around them, and Rose's voice so soft Megan had to lean closer to hear her.

"How do you know when someone is The One? Can anyone really ever be completely sure?"

Megan glanced around to see if anyone else had heard. Her eyes met Caleb's, and the world stopped for a moment – Megan heard nothing and saw no one else for that one long moment, and the pieces of her heart sputtered as his green eyes stared back at her.

She looked away first, knowing if she didn't, she would collapse.

Megan turned back to Rose. "I wish I knew the answer, but my best guess is that we try to find someone who will love us as we are, who we love as they are, and who we can grow with. Life is both messy and fun, you know? You want someone you can do both parts with."

Megan had to force herself not to look at Caleb again. She could feel his gaze on her, like a brand. She doubted she'd ever find anyone else who made her feel like he did.

Later. She'd think about that later.

CHAPTER 12

Her alarm went off and Megan groaned. Another night of restlessness followed by a day jammed with nonstop things to do. Of course.

Henry had said his goodbyes to Rose last night, after dessert, and left to spend his last night as a bachelor at his parents' house.

The plan was for the groomsmen to meet there and get ready before heading to the church.

Meanwhile, the bridesmaids had made camp in the kitchen and dining room. Two makeup artists and two hair stylists had arrived at exactly eight a.m. and were steadily working their way through the bridesmaids.

Megan was first to get her hair done. She'd asked for it up in a simple but elegant bun with the hairclips that Rose had gifted the bridesmaids. She snacked on some of the fruit and crackers on the island counter and watched the hustle and bustle around her.

Ainsley's hair was finished, and she came to stand next to Megan.

"Exciting day, isn't it?" Ainsley side-eyed the crackers on Megan's plate and grabbed some fruit for herself.

"Very exciting. I'm happy for Rose."

"I wonder which of us bridesmaids is going to catch the bouquet." There was a hint of something in Ainsley's voice, as if she was fishing for information.

"I don't know. I hadn't thought about the bouquet toss."

Ainsley turned so her back was to the rest of the bridesmaids and stylists before she responded. "Really? Considering how hot and heavy you and Caleb have been all week, and goodness knows for how long before this week, I'd have thought you'd have plans to knock us all over and catch it – and Caleb."

Megan's blood boiled. She didn't bother keeping the venom out of her voice as she said with a smile, "Good thing it's none of your business. It would be such a shame for a busybody like you to be kept out of the loop, wouldn't it?"

Megan left before Ainsley could say anything else. She sat in the empty chair in front of the makeup artist, who introduced herself as Christine and asked if Megan had any look in mind.

"I think something natural, but I'd love your input."

"Hmm," Christine said. "How do you feel about a sparkly eye shadow to match or complement your dress and a slightly bolder-than-natural lip color?"

Grateful for the distraction, Megan kept the conversation going and asked Christine a few questions about her business.

"I'm actually about to open my own small space in a mall. It's not very big, but gotta start somewhere, right?"

"Launching a project like that is hard. That's amazing."

Christine blushed and finished the last touches of Megan's makeup. Megan wished her luck with her new storefront, gave her a large tip, and took a business card.

Rose wasn't anywhere to be found, and everyone else was either eating or getting glammed up. Megan slipped out of the room and climbed the steps to get dressed, wanting a few minutes to herself.

If Ainsley knew about Megan and Caleb, she must have been the reason Tucker had come looking the other night.

Megan locked the door behind her and got the dress ready and changed into the proper undergarments.

Even if Ainsley only suspected something between Megan and Caleb… Ainsley had always been the jealous type and she must have been pissed by Caleb's casual rejection of her flirtatious behavior. Rejection wasn't something Ainsley handled well.

Even with that aside, why hadn't Caleb fought for her at any point over the years? Not that she'd done any better with her own fear of his rejection.

Megan knew there was only one way to get the answers she needed. But the thought of facing Caleb and having that discussion was too overwhelming and made it difficult to breathe. Of course, that could have been the slightly too tight shapeware. The only reason she wore it was to make sure the dress didn't show any unusual lines – otherwise she believed shapeware to be the work of a masochist.

She slipped on the green tea-length dress and adjusted how everything fit and zipped it closed. Megan was so glad Rose had chosen a style with a side zipper. So much more convenient.

One last check in the mirror and Megan grabbed her heels. She refused to put them on until it was time for photos, opting for socks over her stockings until then.

She met Theresa at the stairs. "Have you seen Rose?" Theresa asked. "The photographer is here."

"No, let me go check her room."

"Thanks – I'm going to go snack. I'm starving."

Megan turned and followed the hall to the second short staircase that led to a converted attic. Rose and Henry had been using it as their bridal suite for the week.

CHAPTER 13

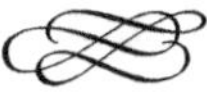

Megan knocked on the door to Rose's room and waited for her cousin to give permission to go in.

She didn't expect to see Rose on the floor with her wedding dress crumpled around her.

Rose looked up at her, her tear-stained face red. "Megan, I can't marry him."

"Oh, Rose." Megan sat next to her cousin and put a hand on her shoulder. "What happened?"

Rose sniffled and looked away. "Nothing happened. I don't think I love him enough to marry him."

That didn't make sense. Not after spending almost an entire week celebrating Rose and Henry. Still, Megan tried for supportive instead of confused.

"Honey, what does that mean?"

Rose wiped away tears. "Do you remember Jacob Clark?"

The name was familiar, but it took Megan a few moments to place it. "Not really. He was your high school boyfriend, right? What does he have to –" Understanding washed over Megan. "You're still in love with Jacob."

Rose only nodded.

"But it's been years since you've seen him. How could you possibly know that you love him?"

"I saw him two weeks ago." Rose glanced at Megan and then away again. "Nothing happened. We ran into each other at the store and talked for a little. I haven't been able to stop thinking about him, but all the feelings are still there."

That didn't seem like enough to call off an entire future with someone else, but Megan wasn't in a position to argue the point.

"Does he know?

Rose shook her head. "I doubt it."

"So, the wedding today is…off?" Megan tried to sound non-judgmental, and she really didn't blame Rose for anything. Her timing could have been better, considering the limo to take the bridal party to the church was already idling outside.

"I don't know."

Megan put her hand on Rose's shoulder and gave a quick squeeze. "Honey, if it's not a 'hell yes, I'm going to marry that man,' there should be no wedding. Even when there aren't feelings for another man involved."

Rose turned to face her and took a deep breath. "It's off." Rose's shoulders dropped and she started to cry again. "What do I do now? Everyone is coming today. How am I supposed to tell them there won't be a wedding?" Rose's voice started to squeak in panic, and Megan went into mom-friend anxiety override.

"You're not. *You* are going to go home." She held up a hand as Rose started to protest. "No, not your apartment with Henry. You can crash at my place if you don't want to go to your parents' house. Pack a bag and go. You can sleep in my bed if you want. Handle the rest of it later. *I* will go to the church and talk to everyone, except Henry. That is for you to handle. I'm sorry."

"What about everything else?"

"I'll handle wedding cleanup. Let's get you out of the dress and into something comfortable, yeah?" Megan stood and held her hands out. Rose hesitated for a few heartbeats and then let

Megan hoist her into a standing position. Megan tried not to topple backwards as Rose threw her arms around Megan's neck.

"Thank you."

Megan hugged her cousin back. "Any time, Rose."

They worked together to get Rose out of the white ball of tulle and lace and into a pair of leggings and a shirt. Most of Rose's things were already packed in preparation for the honeymoon, so it didn't take long to get her loaded into a car with the key to Megan's apartment. Megan stood by the limo and watched as her cousin drove away.

Summoning every ounce of courage, Megan turned to the driver. "It's just me, I guess."

The limo pulled up to the red brick church ten minutes later. Caleb stood outside, his suit pressed, and jacket buttoned. The only word that came to Megan's mind was 'dashing.' He looked dashing. He'd turned in her direction as the limo pulled up in front of the steps, confusion tugging his features when she was the only one who got out of the back.

"Megs – Megan. Where's Rose?"

She took a shaky breath and shook her head, words failing her completely. Caleb's face paled, but he held out his arm to help her up the steps to the entrance. Megan didn't want to let go of him yet, so she let him give her support.

Caleb reached for the door, but Megan held him back. "Wait, don't open it yet. I don't know what to say."

"To Henry?"

She nodded. "And to everyone else. Rose is going to have to talk to Henry at some point and will have to handle the fallout from this. But right now, it's on me to tell everyone in there that the bride isn't coming and there will be no happily-ever-after today."

Caleb stepped in front of her and used his finger to tilt her chin up. The concern was clear in his green eyes. Megan waited for a heartbeat. Waited for him to see her fear, to see the truth. She loved him but what if it wasn't enough? What if his feelings were still malleable enough to be scared away again? What if he didn't stay?

He must have seen the questions in her expression because he gave her a sad smile. "I'll pull Henry aside and tell him she's not coming."

If Rose couldn't marry Henry – if Rose, who had seemed so in love and so sure of her decision until this morning, couldn't go through with the wedding, then what chance did she and Caleb stand?

Things were so complicated. If it was meant to be, should it be so terrifying? Shouldn't there be some level of certainty?

As they stood outside the door, his fingers lingering on her chin, Megan searched Caleb's eyes, his face, for any sign of how he felt, of what was on his mind.

"Are you ready?" Caleb's voice was soft, and he dropped his hand back to his side.

No. "Yes, I'm ready." She still had no idea what she was going to tell everyone, but as Caleb opened the door, Megan stepped into the church with her heart breaking – for herself or for Rose, she couldn't tell.

CHAPTER 14

An hour later, Megan was back at her family's farmhouse. She stood outside in the late-afternoon sun, head tilted up to the sky, and soaked up the warmth. She still wore the light green dress but had kicked off her heels to stand barefoot in the grass.

She knew the moment she stepped inside to pack the rest of her things and load them into her car reality would sink back in, and she wasn't in a hurry for that to happen. Rose had texted to let Megan know she'd arrived safely at Megan's apartment but wouldn't be staying the night – she wanted to talk to Henry and explain and then would stay at her parents' house.

Selfish as it was, Megan was thankful Rose decided not to stay. Megan had her own emotional baggage to unpack and sort through, and it was time she finally faced it.

This last week with Caleb was a fever dream, a fantasy come to life. Until reality had crashed into them and held up a mirror to show it was nothing more than bad decisions.

She didn't know how she would let Caleb go, how to open her hand and let the image of them happy together blow away into the ether. A piece of her heart would always belong to him.

"You really like to keep a man waiting, don't you, Megs?"

Megan whirled to find Caleb leaning against the doorway to the farmhouse, arms crossed. Caleb still wore the dress shirt and slacks, but the top two buttons of the shirt were undone, and his tie was loose around his neck and hung down his chest.

"I –" Megan didn't have anything to say. She hadn't expected to find him here. There was no car parked in the driveway except hers. She wasn't ready for this conversation, had hoped to have it later – over the phone. It was hard enough to decide not to continue things between them, but the thought of ending things with him in person was too much to bear. "What are you doing here?"

"Waiting for you." He didn't move a muscle, but every single ounce of his attention was focused on her.

"Why?"

"I was worried."

She wanted nothing more than to melt into his arms and let him comfort her after having to cancel her cousin's wedding…on the morning of the wedding, at the church. But instead, she grabbed her shoes from the grass a few feet away and stepped onto the wraparound porch.

"I'm fine. I came to get my things. You can go."

"I don't think so." He pushed off the doorway and blocked her path into the house.

Megan halted, her breath coming out in a huff. His arrogance grated on her already thin nerves. "Excuse me?"

"Megs, you don't get to shove me away right now."

"Stop calling me that." She made to go inside but he didn't budge. She should know better than to think he would simply move out of her way. No, Caleb had always been in her way in one shape or form.

"Will you listen for once?"

Outrage bubbled in her chest and throat, and she went to tell him where to shove it, but he cut her off.

"I was wrong. I should never have listened to Tucker. I should never have stayed away. I didn't think you felt the same way. Not until our first night together, all those years ago. But then…" Caleb trailed off.

"Then you left," Megan finished for him.

"Yes. Do you hate me for that? For pursuing my goal?" Incredulity laced his voice and flashed across his face.

"I don't hate you at all." She fought back tears. "That's part of the problem." Her voice broke and she forced herself to finish her thought. "I have never hated you, Caleb."

He reached for her again. Megan let him take her hand. It was an effort to keep it from shaking.

"Why did you never say anything?" she whispered.

Caleb took a deep breath and met her gaze. "It never seemed like the right time," he started. "And you're my best friend's younger sister. I didn't want to hurt you."

Megan tried to pull away, but he held tighter.

"I was afraid."

She snapped her head up at his admission, at the vulnerability in his voice. It made her heart ache.

"Of Tucker?"

"No. I understood what he thought he was doing and used it as an excuse instead of facing the real reason, like a coward."

Megan squeezed his hand. "What is the real reason?"

"I love you. I've loved you for a decade, Megs."

Her heart beat so hard Megan thought it would crack her ribs. But she still needed an explanation. "Then why did you never say anything? What were you afraid of?"

"I don't have parents who had a happy marriage. They were miserable when they were together and have continued to hate each other even after the divorce. I thought that's what happened to marriage – divorce." The catch in his voice broke her heart. "I never wanted to hate you, Megs."

"That's why you stayed away."

He nodded.

"What changed?"

"I love you." He smiled, as if it answered everything.

"I don't know what to say."

"Megan, I love you. I was young and stupid and didn't know any better. That night together last month changed everything for me. I realized how much of an idiot I've been and how unhappy I've been for years. When my uncle offered me the store, he told me how proud he was of the man I'd become, how different from my father I was. It was what I needed to hear to figure out I can do things differently. Their marriage was the exception, not the rule.

"I want you, Megan. I've always wanted you. I will always want you. You are the most incredible, brave, infuriating, intelligent woman I've ever known. I want to spend my life at your side as you conquer anything and everything."

Megan didn't bother to wipe away the tears that now fell freely. "What if I can't conquer anything?" she whispered.

Caleb smiled, his gaze never leaving hers. "I'll be there with ice cream and a shoulder to lean on." He squeezed her hands. "Megs, I just want to be yours."

Megan let the words settle and waited for fear or disbelief to appear in her gut. Nothing – only hope and happiness bloomed in her heart.

She grinned up at him and stared into his green eyes as she said, "I love you, too." It was so simple and the purest truth.

EPILOGUE

The three boxes of cookies, brownies, and cupcakes teetered in Megan's arms as she waited for Caleb to open the door. Recently renamed, Starfire Lake Books was hosting the first ever Halloween Books and Bash for local kids and teens. In fact, two parties in one day.

The first party was just before noon, for all the kids not yet in school. The second party would start at five and go until nine tonight. Caleb had spent months planning and preparing for both parties, doing his best to leave nobody out.

Megan had gotten up at an ungodly hour to make sure the cupcakes were decorated, and the brownies wrapped individually. The sun had only just come up a few minutes earlier, but the rain had started overnight and had turned into a deluge just as she'd finished loading the boxes into the back of her SUV.

Megan was grateful for the awning over the front of the store. Caleb appeared and opened the door. Megan slipped inside.

"Hey, Megs," he gave her a quick kiss as he took the boxes from her. "Are there more in the car?"

"Yes, in the trunk. I'll be right back," she said.

"No, I'll get them in a minute. Come in and dry off."

The soft light shimmered on Megan's engagement ring as she locked the door behind them.

Megan couldn't stop her smile as she followed Caleb to the back storage room. The books were a familiar sight, but she took in the Halloween decorations. There were bats, ghosts, and even a couple of witches riding broomsticks strung up from the ceiling all throughout. A few plastic skeletons hid among the aisles of books in the teen and adult sections.

There were colorfully painted pumpkins in the kid's area, with at least five plastic bins of tiny pumpkins stacked against the wall.

"What are the little pumpkins for?" she asked Caleb as they passed.

"Painting for the little kids. There's a few boxes of paint in the back room."

"Is that why Tony asked me about pumpkins last week when I dropped off their order at the farm?" Tony McCulloh and his wife Sarah had taken over his family's farm, Willowwood Farms, over the summer. Megan opened the storeroom door and held it as Caleb eased his way through with the boxes.

"Yep. He called me after to confirm how many pumpkins I needed."

"I told him you were the person to ask. Anyway, the decorations look great, Caleb. What time did you come home last night?" Megan had given up fighting her heavy eyes just after midnight.

"Around one. You were already asleep."

Megan stuck her tongue out at him as she sorted the boxes and made sure the desserts were still intact. There were a few bumps on the roads to the store from their house. She still had trouble believing they lived together. "What time did you get up?"

"Five thirty. I still have a lot to do."

Satisfied all the desserts were safe, Megan closed the boxes again and asked, "What can I do to help?"

"If you want to get the painting supplies out of the boxes in here, that would be great." He pulled her in for a too-short kiss.

"No problem. Rose is going to meet me here before we meet Abbie for breakfast at the diner." The Starfire Lake Diner had the best omelets in town. The three of them got together as often as possible, which hadn't been much lately, so Megan was excited to catch up and chat with her best friend and her cousin. "I'll bring something back for you."

Caleb blew her a kiss before he went to get the rest of the desserts. There were more at the house. In fact, the kitchen and dining area had been taken over by cupcakes, brownies, and cookies shaped like the usual Halloween favorites: ghosts, pumpkins, and black cats. Megan would bring them later that afternoon before the second party.

Megan spent the next hour organizing the painting supplies while Caleb hung more decorations and made sure the store was ready to open.

In the last year, Caleb had transformed the store from struggling to thriving, and still found the energy to support her in her own endeavor to open a bakery.

The storefront she'd originally wanted had fallen through, but her realtor found one that was even closer to the bookstore and the heart of town. Renovations were underway, and she had plans to stop there after breakfast to talk to the contractor about the schedule.

A knock at the front door made her jump and drop the paint sets in her hands. Megan cursed but was glad the lids were so secure. She peeked over the shelves and saw Rose. Megan ignored the scattered plastic kits around her and went to let Rose inside.

"Hey!" Megan hugged her cousin and locked the door behind her.

"It's insane out there. I haven't seen so much rain in a while," Rose said. Megan led the way back to the kid's area and cleaned up the extra paint kits and set them aside. She had also set up a table with an orange tablecloth and set up the pumpkin-themed paper plates, cups, and napkins.

"I hope it stops before the party. Caleb worked so hard to set it up, I don't want people to skip it because of the rain." Megan glanced out the giant front windows. She watched as a car drove through a puddle and a wave of water splashed up.

"I think it's going to stop before then. The place looks great! The kids are going to love it."

Megan smiled and pride swelled as she looked around at the decorated store. "I think so, too." She laughed as she said, "I don't know who is going to be more excited – the kids or Caleb."

Megan grabbed her things from the storage room and met Megan at the front door. Caleb was nowhere to be found, so she sent him a quick text message to tell him that she'd be back later.

The diner wasn't too crowded yet. There were a few customers finishing up their breakfast, but it was the perfect lull between those who had to be at work and those who started their day later.

Abbie was already in one of the back booths and waved her arm as she spotted Megan and Rose. Megan scooted in to sit next to the window and Rose slid in next to her.

"I ordered everyone coffee, it'll be here in a second," Abbie said as she handed them menus.

"Great, thanks. I definitely need some." Megan perused the menu, but nothing grabbed her attention the way the thought of an omelet had.

"How is prep for the party going?" Abbie asked.

"Caleb is losing his mind, but the store looks great. He's been so excited that I don't think he's slept all month."

Abbie raised an eyebrow. "Is it just excitement about the party or has something, or should I say some*one,* been keeping him up at all hours of the night?"

Megan didn't blush as she grinned. The memory of the other night flashed through her mind, of Caleb's lips on her skin and his hands on her body. She took a sip from her water glass to battle the flush that came over her at the thoughts.

Abbie laughed, and then turned to Rose. "So, what's new with you?"

Rose put down the menu and sat against the back of the booth. "Not much. Hard to have stuff happen when you're still a social pariah."

Megan met Abbie's glance. It had been over a year since Rose called off her wedding, and neither her family nor Henry's had gotten over it.

"It's ridiculous that Henry's family is still ignoring you," Abbie said.

"I don't blame them," Rose said, a hint of sadness in her voice. "They were excited for Henry and their dynastic future. I ruined it."

Abbie huffed but Megan cut in, "You ruined *their* plans but saved your heart. That's what matters. You were under no obligation to be part of some, how did you put it? Dynastic future. This is the twenty-first century. They're not part of the British aristocracy, for crying out loud."

Rose smiled at her, and Megan saw gratitude in Rose's eyes.

"I know. And part of me is angry that they aren't over it. At least his mom isn't shunning mine at the club anymore. They refuse to sit with me, of course, but that's whatever. I stopped going to club. I've never liked it."

Despina, their waitress, interrupted to deliver their coffees and take their orders. Megan laughed when they each ordered a different omelet and home fries.

After Despina left to put their orders in, Abbie turned to Rose and said, "That family has always been snotty. You deserve in-laws who see you as more than a brood mare for their son to breed."

Rose choked on her coffee and spluttered.

"It wasn't *that* scandalous a thing to say, was it?" Abbie asked.

Megan passed Rose some napkins and helped her clean up the table.

"No, I thought I saw someone," Rose said. Her cheeks were red.

"Who?" Abbie moved closer to the window to look, but Megan knew the answer. She'd seen him walk by, and had a feeling the jingle on the door of the diner meant he had come in.

Jacob Clark. Rose's high school boyfriend. The memory of him and a chance meeting just before she was supposed to walk down the aisle to Henry had been enough for Rose to call off the wedding.

Megan noticed Rose's eyes widen ever so slightly.

"Never mind, I don't think it was hi—her."

Abbie started to say something, but Megan shook her head once. Abbie stopped and took a sip of her coffee instead.

"So, Abbie, what's new with you? How's Derek?" Megan asked. She and Abbie focused on each other and gave Rose the time she needed to compose herself again.

"He's great." There was a dreamy quality in her voice, "He's in Paris for the week for an event and then he'll be home for a couple of months. I'm looking forward to it." Abbie sighed, her head on her hand. "I miss him."

"Looks like Megan won't be the only one up all night," Rose joked.

Megan laughed, and Abbie's face turned bright red.

"Oh, please, Abs. It's not like you to be shy – I do believe you spent a weekend having lots of hot sex with him after you met," Megan said.

"No, it's not that. It's – I haven't slept next to him in months and all I can think about is jumping his bones as soon as he walks in the door."

Rose shrugged. "I don't see why that's a bad thing. Jump on him. Good sex is hard to come by, and great sex even more so."

Megan twisted to look at Rose. "I don't think I've ever heard you talk about sex, Rose."

"I don't, usually. But it's not like I'm wrong."

"No, you're not." Megan wondered if that was one of the reasons Rose had called off the wedding but thought asking seemed impertinent and callous.

"We shouldn't settle, that's all I'm saying," Rose clarified.

"Hmm," was all Megan said. Abbie watched the exchange with the rapt attention of someone taking in an exciting tennis match.

Rose took a long drink of her water. Megan took that to mean the topic was over and they needed to find something new to talk about.

Thankfully, their waitress brought their food over a moment later. It was distraction enough and both Megan and Abbie let the conversation drop.

"Abbie, how is your art coming along?" Rose asked between bites of her omelet.

"Pretty good. Derek helped me revamp my website and set up a nicer online store, and that's been insane." Abbie blushed.

"That's awesome. Good for you," Rose raised her coffee mug. Megan followed suit, and then Abbie lifted hers and they all clinked mugs and took a sip.

"Proud of you, Abs," Megan said.

A little more than hour later, Megan was back at home and in the kitchen to finish decorating the goodies for the second party at the bookstore. She'd convinced Caleb to have a delayed opening this morning, but the sound of his truck in the driveway surprised her.

The front door opened and closed, and she heard Caleb call out for her.

"I'm in the kitchen," she said. The piping bag was still in her hand as Caleb wrapped his arms around her middle and buried his face in the crook of her neck.

"You smell delicious." The growl in his words made her heart race.

Megan put the icing down and turned around in his arms. "I smell like icing and chocolate." She put her hands around his neck and kissed him. His lips were soft, and she groaned at the taste of him.

Caleb moved his hands to her ass and lifted her. She wrapped her legs around him as he carried her to the couch. He sat down and she adjusted her position on his lap, her knees to either side of him. The desire in his green eyes was matched by her own, but there was softness in his eyes, too.

He traced his fingers along her back. Megan closed her eyes and let her world narrow to the two of them. In that moment, nothing else mattered.

"Megs?"

"Hmm?" She opened her eyes and took in the quiet strength and rugged handsomeness of him. He'd let his hair grow out a couple of inches – not long enough to require a lot of maintenance but just enough so she could wrap her fingers in it when his head was between her legs.

"Thank you." He brushed a loose strand of hair out of her face and tucked it behind her ear. Her heart warmed at the gesture.

"For what?"

Caleb held her left hand in his and brushed his thumb against the three stone-engagement ring he'd given her the week before. "Giving me the chance to be yours."

Tears sprung in her eyes, and she did her best to hold them back. "I love you, Caleb."

"To the moon and back, princess."

If you like second-chance romances with a touch of wit and a lot of steam, check out Rose and Jacob's story in WICKED TEMPTATION!

ACKNOWLEDGMENTS

Husband – thank you for being mine, and for loving me as I am. I'm glad I get to be yours and you get to be mine.

Chipmunk – Mama loves you so much. You are such a sweet, funny, smart, strong little kid and I am so lucky to be your mama.

Wifey – I couldn't do this (or life) without you. As a very wise fictional character said, "Family don't end in blood."

Melissa Wolfe – Thank you for being a friend!

Blue Saffire – Look, I did it again!

My writing community – Jeannie Moon, Patty Blount, Zoe York, Carrie Lomax, Stacey Agdern, Jayne Rylon, Eve Pendle, Brighton Walsh, Katie Lillig, Kate Nolan, Lexi Ryan: I couldn't do any of this without you. Your experience and wisdom and willingness to share both with a new author like me is astounding and I don't have words to convey my appreciation.

Holland Rae – My late-night writing buddy, I don't know what I'd do without your support and help.

Rebecca – Thank you for your help with this book. Megan and Caleb's story is so much better because of it!

Kristina P. – Proofreader extraordinaire, thank you! I'd like to note that any typos or mistakes in this book are my own and probably because I ignored her advice.

Naomi Lane – Thank you for putting up with me changing my mind a bunch of times before the cover was perfect! Give your fur babies kisses from me!

Bellevue Crew – Couldn't do this Mom thing without ya'll.

My family and friends – I love you all so much and appreciate your encouragement and support!

Nyx & Lila – you two are my best buddies, and I couldn't get through the day without you. Thank you for loving Chipmunk as much as you do and being the best older furry siblings to him. I love you both, and writing wouldn't be the same without your company.

My readers - thank you. I hope you liked the book, but I also know not every book is going to be everyone's cup of tea. It doesn't matter if you're a new-to-me reader or someone who has read one of my other books, thank you for giving this story a chance.

ABOUT THE AUTHOR

Though she grew up on Long Island, Vivi Parish now lives in the suburbs of Texas with her husband, toddler, and two very sweet dogs. You can find Vivi active on social media posting photos of her dogs and daily life.

Be sure to sign up for her newsletter for book updates. You can find her on social media here.

Her website is www.viviparish.com.

9 798985 940831